PRAIRIE CHARM

PRIMROSE SERIES

BOOK NINE

TANYA RENEE

Serenade Publishing

www.serenadepublishing.com

For my soul sister and awesome friend, Mandi. Here's your silver fox!

ALSO BY TANYA RENEE

Primrose Series

Prairie Sky

Prairie Nights

Prairie Fire

Prairie Hearts

Prairie Sound

Prairie Rain

Prairie Prestige

Prairie Roads

Prairie Charm

Prairie Rose

With The Band

Finding Direction

Love Notes

On The Edge Of Forever

PROLOGUE

It had been a long day. Dinner service was now over; the kitchen cleaned to pristine perfection and ready for another insane day. Falyn leaned against the stainless-steel countertop, her feet burning and back aching from slaving over the hot stove. Nodding her goodbyes to her sous chefs and kitchen staff, she watched them leave out the back door When all was quiet, she inhaled deeply, proud of another successful night at the restaurant. Glancing around the now empty kitchen, she smiled. The large commercial space for their posh eatery, a dream to cook in.

Her thoughts drifted to Pierre, her handsome restaurateur husband of seven years, who built this kitchen with her needs in mind and used it to not only persuade her to be his Executive Chef but also his devoted wife. They had become a team, making La Fleur one of the most popular French bistros in the trendy and historic neighborhood of Gastown in Vancouver. With its fresh takes on classic French cuisine, superior curated wine list, dark, moody lighting, and swanky décor, it was a hot spot and, without question, one of the most sought-after restaurant reservations on a Saturday night.

Falyn slipped into the office, reached for her jacket and grabbed her purse, stopping a moment to take in the wedding photo of her and Pierre sitting next to his computer. She frowned. *No texts from Pierre.* She was hoping to hear from him. A sweet little 'I love you' or 'how did the night go' at the very least. It wasn't too much to ask. Just a text to say he was thinking of her. Like the old days when they were first married and before life became complicated and far too busy.

She sighed, pushing through the kitchen door. She entered the darkened dining room, the only light illuminating her way from the back light of the glass bar shelving. Falyn ran her hand over the elegant, smooth surface of the marble bar top and glanced around the empty restaurant. She loved this time of night when no one was around; the silence was a welcome reprieve from the craziness of the night. A brief moment of peace before going home. *Home.* An unexpected wave of homesickness washed over her as she thought about her hometown. La Fleur was a far cry from the greasy diners of small-town Manitoba that started her culinary passion. A nostalgic smile tipped up Falyn's lips as she thought about flipping burgers at her first cooking job at the Eazy Café in Primrose, Manitoba. *If only they could see me now.*

With a reminiscent smile, Falyn reached the door, taking one last look around as her phone chimed with a text from her Uber driver telling her he had arrived.

Exiting the building, she locked the door behind her and climbed into the car, giving the driver her address.

Pierre had gone home earlier, right after dinner service, stating he was exhausted and had phone calls to make regarding a potential second restaurant he was considering opening in Fairview along the waterfront. She admired his drive and resourcefulness and couldn't wait to see what he had planned for their next venture.

Falyn rested her head back against the leather of the backseat, thinking about the soothing bath she was going to soak in when she got home and about climbing into her warm, soft bed with Pierre. Keeping the same hours as her, Pierre was likely still awake, and she couldn't wait to run her hands through his dark hair and get seduced by his sultry brown eyes and smooth, handsome face. Despite her exhaustion, he would inevitably pin her to the mattress with his hard, lean body and coax her into having sex. She would protest, but eventually give in, getting swept up in Pierre's passionate embrace. Her husband had a ravenous appetite in the bedroom, and she was sure it was normal for a couple, especially a couple as busy as they were, to simply fall asleep at the end of a long night wrapped in each other's arms. Yet if she denied his seduction, Pierre would pout, saying the spark wasn't what it used to be and asking where it had all gone wrong. Her European-born French husband was dramatic with a capital D, and some days that was part of what added to her overall exhaustion.

Arriving home, she paid the Uber driver, exited the car and entered their posh apartment building. Greeting the night security with a wave, she made her way to the elevator. Before she could press the up button, the elevator chimed and a young, raven-haired woman quickly exited the elevator. Dressed in a red figure-hugging dress and sky-high designer heels, she was beautiful and modelesque, standing at least six inches taller than Falyn's petite frame. The younger woman, obviously in a hurry, didn't notice her at first and nearly knocked Falyn over as she hurried out of the elevator. Finally, noticing her, she met Falyn's surprised gaze, her red painted lips smudged at the edges, and instantly Falyn recognized her as one of the hostesses at La Fleur.

"Oh, hi!" Falyn exclaimed as the woman stopped dead in her tracks, both recognition and trepidation in her eyes.

The young woman's dark eyes grew wide, and she went to open her mouth but instead closed it tightly and hurried out of the building, leaving a trail of her floral perfume and Falyn standing there completely bewildered by her reaction. *What the hell was that?* Falyn frowned and shook her head as she climbed onto the elevator and pressed the penthouse floor button. When the doors opened, Pierre was there, leaning against the opening shirtless and in silk pajama pants slung low on his narrow hips.

"There's my gorgeous wife," he said, his hands sliding around her waist to her behind and giving it a squeeze. "I've been waiting for you."

Falyn smiled, not sure she had the energy for his flirtation and what that led to, but choosing to give in. Pierre leaned in, capturing her lips in a scorching kiss. He tasted like red wine, and she melted against his embrace, her exhausted body protesting as she did. Pulling away from him, she gave Pierre a weary look.

"It's been an exhausting day, Pierre. Can we rain check till the morning? All I want is a hot bath, then to curl up into bed and fall asleep."

"Whatever you need, babe," he said uncharacteristically agreeable as he released her so she could walk past him towards the bedroom down the hall. When she entered her room, he went straight for her dresser, pulling out a slinky silk chemise that he had bought her recently and she had yet to wear. Falyn frowned at it, wishing he had grabbed her cozy cotton pajamas instead. She didn't have the energy to say anything, so she collapsed onto the soft down comforter.

Pierre let out a sardonic laugh and jutted out his bottom lip teasingly. "Oh, my poor petite cracheur de feu." He sauntered over to her, giving her his sexiest bedroom eyes, and she groaned as she reached for her pillow, burying her face in it. She inhaled deeply, expecting to smell the lavender laundry soap she always used, but instead, a familiar rich floral scent assaulted her nose. Her eyes widened as she turned and bolted upright, discarding the pillow to her side.

"What's wrong, baby? Have you changed your mind and are going to let me have my way with you?" he asked with a low chuckle as he leaned in to kiss her.

Her hand came up, bracing against Pierre's bare chest as her eyes flitted to the side table where a lone wine glass stood, the rim painted in traitorous red lipstick.

CHAPTER 1

Falyn gazed out over the Prairie Charm Bed and Breakfast property, taking in the huge, castle-like house that oozed country character. The house was charming, just as the worn-out wooden sign next to the door indicated, and Falyn smiled. The For Sale sign creaked as it swung back and forth in the winter wind, and Falyn pulled down her toque over her ears and wrapped her arms around herself as her eyes drifted over to the smaller cottage tucked towards the back of the property. It was European in style, cute and quaint, and a perfect little home for her to start her new life in.

A new life. Never did she think she would be here, both back in Primrose and in this limbo place in her life. Her seven years of seemingly contented marriage ended so unceremoniously that she hardly had time to process. After she caught Pierre cheating and sifted through his years of lies and betrayal, their divorce went smoothly, all things considered. Of course, the reason Pierre was as amicable as he was, pushing for the divorce to be finalized, was because his mistress, almost 20 years his junior, was expecting their first baby. The news hit Falyn like a direct kick to the gut of her already fragile psyche. She and Pierre had decided that children didn't fit into their long-term plans and goals of owning a chain of high-end restaurants. The "bust your ass" lifestyle wouldn't allow for it. And in many ways, at the time she agreed. As a chef, it was hard to juggle the long, late hours with a family, and when she and Pierre got together, she accepted the fact that to be with him would mean she had to sacrifice. Now, at 32, divorced and childless, she wished she had made other choices.

Falyn sighed and glanced at the For Sale sign. This was her opportunity to build something that was truly hers and start over in a place that, no matter where she was in this world, always felt like home. Primrose, Manitoba was a small town 30 minutes from the provincial capital of Winnipeg. It was thriving with a resurgence of businesses and development over the past ten years and had become a haven for those wanting to escape the big cities with its small-town charm and slower-paced lifestyle. With her substantial divorce settlement now in her account, she not only had the money to buy this property, but the money to renovate the bed and breakfast and the cottage to her liking.

The sound of a car horn startled her from her thoughts as her realtor, Saige Runo, pulled in next to her car. Saige exited the vehicle, her long strawberry blonde hair blowing in the winter wind, her smile wide as she waved to Falyn and strode over to her with a portfolio in her hands. Falyn lifted her hand to wave back, happy to see her high school friend again after so many years.

"Falyn! Oh my gosh, you look fantastic! Seriously, how long has it been? Ten years at least, can you believe it!" Saige exclaimed as she wrapped her in a friendly hug.

Falyn laughed, not expecting such a warm personal welcome, almost forgetting how friendly everyone was in a small town. Saige let go of her, and Falyn couldn't help but grin at her old friend.

Saige Runo was a Primrose resident, top realtor in the area, a dynamo at design, and every bit the effervescent personality she remembered from high school. Saige tossed her perfectly styled long hair behind her, wrapped her arm around Falyn's shoulder and turned to face the large guest house in front of them. "What do you think?" she asked. "Has it got potential or what?"

"It sure does." Falyn agreed with a nod. "What in terms of renovations do you think I would be looking at?"

"A new roof for sure, but other than that, mostly aesthetic changes. It needs to be brought up to date a bit, but the bones are fantastic and the kitchen, well, let's just say, I don't cook but the kitchen makes me want to learn." she said with a cheeky grin and a wink. "Let's go inside and check it out. I truly think you will fall in love."

The women made their way to the front door. Saige pulled out the key, turned the lock, and met Falyn's gaze with a big, bright smile as she slowly opened the door and said, "Welcome to Prairie Charm."

* * *

Falyn pulled onto her parents' driveway, seeing the old white two-story farmhouse she grew up in. Getting out of her car, she was literally vibrating with excitement to tell her parents the great news as she strode towards the front door.

"Hey there, Cookie!" The gruff voice of her father sounded behind her. She turned, seeing the round, weathered face of her father, Duncan Isley, decked out in his usual barn coveralls, his favorite Hastings Hardware hat on his head and big muck boots on his feet.

"Hey Dad!" she replied, slipping her arm around his thick waist and curling up her nose. "You stink. Coming in from the barn?"

"Yep. Just checking on my hens. Egg production is down with this cold weather, but I have them nice and cozy under the lamps," he said, lifting the pail he had in his hand for Falyn to see. Inside the pail were approximately five dozen eggs. "We usually get more, but those girls need warmth to produce."

Falyn laughed at the way her father babied his chickens. The man was a farmer through and through and loved not only the lifestyle of farming but the science behind it all. If you wanted to get into her father's good graces, all you had to do was ask him about his chickens, and suddenly you were best friends. There was nothing like farm-fresh eggs, and Falyn was without question going to take advantage of this connection in the future.

The wind whipped up, causing a small snow squall to swirl around them, and Falyn shivered, gripping the lapel of her wool coat.

"Let's get out of this wind," her father said, opening the front door.

Falyn and her father slipped inside the front porch where her father shed his coveralls and boots and stepped inside the house. The heavenly smell of freshly baked chocolate chip cookies wafted from the kitchen. Falyn breathed deeply, the familiar, comforting scent reminding her of all the times she and her brother, Brooks, came home from school after her mother had baked their favorite treat. Removing her jacket, boots and toque, she hung them on the hooks by the door and made her way into the farmhouse kitchen. The space was small and cozy; the cabinets were plain and painted white to give the illusion of openness. Off white laminate countertops that were chipped and scratched created an L shape and housed exactly two small appliances on the counters. A coffee maker and a toaster. A small microwave stood in the corner on its own stand that also acted as a bookshelf for her mother's well-loved cookbook collection. A modest rectangular pine table took up most of the remaining space, seating four comfortably and six if in a pinch for a family dinner.

Her mother, Dorothy Isley, was at the stove with a cheerful, frilly, floral apron around her waist and was humming to an old Reba McEntire tune that was playing on a little radio that sat on the window ledge. She was transferring cookies onto a wire cooling rack with a spatula in hand.

"Smells amazing in here." Falyn said as she approached her mother and planted a kiss on her cheek. Her mother beamed, her round, red-cheeked face bright and welcoming. Her snow white shoulder length curly hair was pulled back at the sides with comb clips, and her blue eyes sparkled at the sight of her daughter.

"I've been waiting for you. How was the property?" she asked, her attention returning to lifting cookies off the sheet pans.

"It was amazing," Falyn replied with a contented sigh as she pulled a glass out of the cupboard then opened the refrigerator, pulling out the jug of milk. Her father gestured for her to pour him a glass too, and once she had two tall glasses of cold milk poured, she returned the jug to the refrigerator.

Taking a seat at the table, she handed the second glass to her father and reached for a cooled chocolate chip cookie on the platter that was set on the table. Dunking her cookie in the milk, she bit into it, her eyes rolling back with appreciation. "Mom, you still bake the best cookies."

Her mother offered her an appreciative smile as she transferred more cookies onto the platter. "Tell us more. Are you going to put in an offer?"

"Already done," Falyn replied. "The asking price was under my budget, so I offered them a full-price cash offer. The best part is I'll have more than enough money to renovate and decorate."

"I'm proud of you, Cookie," her father said as he leaned back against his chair. "I know Primrose isn't exactly what you're used to anymore, but I can't think of anyone better to take over that property and make Prairie Charm Bed and Breakfast a thriving business again. If there was anything good that came out of your marriage to that dipshit, it's at least this."

"Dad!" Falyn chided her father with amusement.

"Sorry, fuck turd," he said with a wink.

"Duncan, watch your mouth," her mother scolded as she strode over to him, patted his face and smiled lovingly down at her husband. "No need to get all vulgar. Calling Pierre a simple idiot will do."

Falyn laughed, amused by her parents' candor and impassioned distaste for her ex-husband. Her parents never did care for Pierre, even when their marriage seemed good. Pierre had only been to Primrose a handful of times; but each time he turned up his nose at her family and her hometown. Pierre was all about the city and couldn't imagine life beyond the cityscape. The few times he did visit, he would balk at her parent's aged farmhouse and small poultry farm and always brag that he turned his simple hick wife into a sophisticated city girl. That should have been her first clue to bolt in the other direction.

"I'm going to call Jaxon to do an inspection and Saige said she would love to help me decorate once we get to that stage. It's all going to take several months to renovate and get the rooms ready to be rented, but I hope to get it finished by April. That gives me almost five months to restore it to its former glory," she said with a big smile.

"And what about the cottage on the property?" her mother asked, taking a seat with them at the table.

"It's livable. It's small and needs upgrades for sure, but it's cute inside," Falyn replied. "I'm going to work on the big house first so I can get the business running and then work on the cottage. But if my offer is accepted, I'll probably be able to move in before Christmas."

As she said this, her phone chimed with a text. Picking

up her phone, a slow grin curled her lips when she saw Saige's name on the notification. Swiping her phone open, she clicked on her text and beamed as she read: *It's yours.*

* * *

PULLING UP TO PRAIRIE CHARM, Falyn parked her car next to the cottage. Getting out of her vehicle, she opened the back door to retrieve a box of her most prized possessions: her professional knife set along with a few of her favorite pans and utensils to cook with. They were all she had insisted on taking from her kitchen back in Vancouver, and with this box full of kitchen tools, she was sure any meal was possible.

Walking across the yard towards the guest house, trying not to slip on the ice that had formed on the driveway, she made it safely across and carefully strode down the stone walkway to the front door. Falyn glanced at the modest sign that said Prairie Charm Bed and Breakfast. The sign was worn, faded and needed replacing, so she added it to her mental to-do list. Balancing the box with one arm, she unlocked the door and entered the home, her eyes darting around the space. The large front entrance was wide and welcoming, with a large staircase to the second floor and a check-in desk tucked to the side of it. Her eyes drifted around the space, putting herself in the shoes of a potential guest, and she smiled at the thought. Turning, she walked into the great room, featuring a tall, beamed ceiling and a gorgeous stone fireplace. Everything about the room screamed 'come in and sit down', and in her mind's eye she saw multiple seating areas with large, lush furniture that matched the grandness of the room itself. It would have quiet nooks to read and open spaces to socialize. Something for every guest. Off to one end, French doors opened onto a large back patio that overlooked the back lawn. She glanced to the far corner where the ceiling peaked, and she imagined a large Christmas tree, perhaps a Douglas fir, dressed in colorful handmade ornaments from local artisans, curated personally by herself so she could help promote their small businesses. Coming back through the cased opening of the great room, she crossed the front entrance and stepped into the dining room, already furnished with wooden tables and chairs, covered by drop cloths. Having inspected the space earlier, she was happy to find the tables and chairs in good condition to reuse, and she just needed to give them a coat of paint to freshen up their look. There was a long bar-style counter that was perfect for serving up breakfast buffets and space for a coffee and a juice bar. Serving breakfast buffet style wasn't exactly the caliber of the posh dining she was used to, with her fancy culinary training. However, it was cost-effective and would allow her to serve up a variety of delicious offerings that would please everyone. As Falyn was more of a chef than a baker, she had already arranged to outsource decadent baked goods from Marnie Baxter, Primrose's baker extraordinaire and owner of Everything You Knead, located right on Main Street. Glancing around the room, she smiled, almost hearing the happy chatter of guests, the clatter of silverware and the satisfied sighs as they ate the incredible food she had planned: Dishes like brioche French toast, rich Saskatoon buttermilk pancakes, crispy bacon, plump savory sausages and perfectly cooked scrambled eggs sprinkled with fresh herbs. She could almost taste the warm maple syrup. Prairie Charm was going to be a destination not only to stay but to eat, a place that ensured all her guests left well-rested, bellies full, and so charmed they simply had to book their next stay.

Pushing her way through the swinging door of the kitchen, she flipped on the lights, and the large commercial kitchen illuminated. Setting her box down on the stainless-steel island, she glanced around excitedly, taking it all in. If the charm of the house didn't sway her to buy this place, the kitchen certainly would have. With a giant stainless steel prep island taking up the middle of the room, upper floating cabinets lining the walls and deep lower cabinets for storage, along with butcher block counters, she had more than enough space for all the tools and dishes she needed. There was a commercial-grade dishwasher and cold storage tucked into one corner of the room. And the grand dame of the entire kitchen was the large eight-burner gas stove, with a giant overhanging hood vent. It was a dream stove, and Falyn was itching to cook with it. Rummaging through her box, she pulled out her new chef's coat, her name along with Prairie Charm embroidered onto it. A sweet gift from her parents signifying her new start and a bright, exciting future ahead.

The doorbell sounded, breaking Falyn from the endless to-do lists in her head. The chimes sounded like a regal English estate and made her laugh as she exited the kitchen and strode across the dining room to the front door to let in her movers.

CHAPTER 2

Spring had finally arrived in Primrose, and Falyn was grateful. She was no longer used to the cold of a Manitoba winter, realizing how spoiled she was with the milder winters of the West Coast. The past four months had been a whirlwind of activity at Prairie Charm. Having sought advice from her cousin, Jaxon Isley, the owner of Isley Construction, he had inspected the property, finding no structural issues, and had recommended local tradespeople to complete the renovations and aesthetic upgrades. With all the trades lined up, this left her to focus on settling in and planning for the business itself. In five weeks, Prairie Charm was set to open, and Falyn was excited to reveal the new and improved Prairie Charm Bed and Breakfast to her first guests. The word had gotten out, and she was already fully booked for opening weekend and had several dinner events booked, including the wedding rehearsal dinner for her longtime family friend, Kolt Donahue, and his fiancé, Jane. Everything in her business plan was coming together with minimal hiccups.

"Hey, sis." The voice of her brother, Brooks, sounded behind her. "Here you are."

Falyn turned to see her big, strapping younger brother come into the main guest room that was fully renovated and decorated. Her 'little' brother stood six foot three inches tall and was built strong and broad, such a contrast to her petite five-foot four frame. "What do you think? Amazing, right?"

Brooks glanced around, an approving smile painting his face as he took in the fully renovated and decorated bedroom. "It looks fantastic."

"It does, doesn't it?" She answered, taking in the beautiful space. The room was the largest of the six guest rooms and the most private. It was situated at the end of a long hallway and featured an alcove that was part of the spire that graced the outside of the house, making it look like a storybook castle. Against one wall stood a king-size fourposter bed with a tall headboard that had intricately carved roses in the corners. The bed was dressed in crisp white linens and soft, lush-looking pillows. At the end of the bed was a colorful, handmade quilt. Along the side wall stood a long dresser with a mirror that had the same carved roses at the top of the mirror, and a matching armoire stood in the corner.

"Where did you get this furniture?" Brooks asked, walking over to the armoire and running his hands over the detailed carvings. "It's beautiful."

"Believe it or not, it was left here in the house," she replied with a wide smile. "The previous owners took most of the furniture but left the dining room tables and chairs and left all the beds in the rooms. All I had to do was replace the mattresses. This was the only one with a full bedroom set. I loved the furniture the moment I saw it and thought it was perfect with this being Primrose. I asked Hayden if he could make matching headboards for all the other rooms. He said he would have them ready for me next week."

"Nice touch." Brooks replied, nodding his head in approval before turning to meet her gaze. "I actually stopped by here to invite you to the shindig Georgie and I are hosting for our birthdays next weekend."

"When are you going to finally ask that girl out?" Falyn asked, putting her hands on her hips and staring up at her brother incredulously. "Why you two pussyfoot around your feelings is beyond me."

"Well, nosy sister, I would pursue Georgie, but she has made it very clear that she thinks it will ruin our friendship," Brooks replied matter-of-factly, his eyes sparkling with amusement as he continued in a British accent. "So, I shall continue to pine until my fair princess is ready to kiss this toad."

Falyn laughed and swatted her brother on the shoulder. "You're not a toad, Brooks. A little squidgy around the edges," she said, reaching up and mussing his curly hair, "...but definitely not a toad."

"Okay, okay," he said, shifting away from her, then putting his arm around her shoulders. "Let's check out the rest of the house and then I expect some lunch."

She swatted her brother and laughed. "Is that why you're here? To partake in my cooking?"

"Perhaps," he replied with a wink. "But mostly to spend time with my favorite sister."

* * *

IT WAS the night of the birthday celebration for Brooks and Georgie, and Falyn was nervous. It had been years since she had gone to a bar, let alone some honky-tonk bar, filled with wannabe cowboys. *Groan.* The last thing she needed was some young punk in a cowboy hat and boots trying to hit on her over cheap drinks and too loud music. Ten years ago, she may have been game, but not now.

It wasn't lost on Falyn how much she had changed over the past decade. At 32 years old, she had lived in Vancouver most of her adult life and had grown accustomed to the amenities of the big city. When she arrived on the West Coast as a new culinary student, it was such a culture shock from her small-town, country girl upbringing. However, very quickly she acquired a group of friends, mostly in the culinary world, and found herself wrapped up in a lifestyle of fancy wine bars, swanky restaurants, and high-end parties. It was at one of those high-end parties that she met Pierre Beaumont. Pierre was tall, devilishly handsome, dynamic, and had a debonair sexiness with his thick French accent. He came from old money and at 30 was set to open his first restaurant, La Fleur, in a thriving area of downtown Vancouver. The moment their eyes met across the room; Falyn was sure she was going to marry him. Pierre was looking for a young, ambitious sous chef to add to his team and had zoned in on her from their first meeting, very soon offering her not only the job but his bed. Their initial sexual chemistry was amazing, and Falyn found herself completely engulfed by his world within a matter of months. He would call her his "cracheur de feu" or his spitfire, and she ate up every compliment and tidbit of affection he offered.

God, I was stupid. Falyn frowned, emotion rising and causing a lump to constrict painfully in her throat. She closed her eyes and drew in a deep calming breath, repeating until the flood of emotion receded. She had spent too much time crying and wallowing in self-pity over her failed marriage, and she wasn't going to start again now. After she caught Pierre in his lie and he admitted to infidelity, she had done her best to compartmentalize her emotions, and yet when she was alone, truly alone, she let the tears fall. *How can you love someone and hate them at the same time?* Despite her anger and hurt towards Pierre, her traitorous heart still held on to what might have been. *You can't think like that anymore, Falyn.* She needed to move on and forge her own path. Even if the path forward meant she had to walk that path alone.

Falyn took a long, hard look at herself in her mirror and reached up, touching the blonde ringlets of her shoulder-length hair. She liked the way she looked; her eyes were large, a rich dark chocolate brown and expressive. Her lashes were long and dark, eyebrows perfectly arched, and her lips pouty and pink. She had always considered herself pretty, but now as she grew older, she could see the maturity lines and edges forming that weren't there when she moved to Vancouver. Perhaps it was the long, tiring hours of a chef, or the events of the past year that seemed to make them more pronounced, but she didn't like it. Coming back to Primrose was exactly what she needed. A slower pace and no reminders of her previous life with Pierre.

Smoothing down the flowy, long sleeve green blouse she picked out at a shop in St. Augustine, she reached for the dark brown leather cowboy boots that her mother had kept in storage for her when she moved away and slipped them on. Never did she think she would be wearing these boots again. Her boots had stories. Wild and crazy stories of a barely legal age, Falyn, and all the rebellious antics she and her friends got into. Surely things her West Coast self would balk at. But now, this was a new version of Falyn. A stronger, more independent version of herself and perhaps a part of the wild and uninhibited Falyn needed to make a little comeback.

ARRIVING at the infamous Pickled Pig honky-tonk bar on the outskirts of St. Augustine, Falyn parked her car next to Ben and Ever Hastings, who arrived around the same time she did. Big old Ben, as he was lovingly referred to, climbed out of his truck, looking just as brawny and intimidating as he always did. The only thing was that there was nothing intimidating about him other than his stature. He was still the big old teddy bear she remembered. As for his wife, Ever, she hadn't had the chance to get to know her well and had a feeling if she did, they would be fast friends. She, like Falyn, had left the comfort of their small town to pursue her dreams in a big city, and she understood how difficult it was to come back. *I'm definitely going to talk to her tonight.* Ben and Ever greeted her as they joined their group already gathering by the doors of the bar.

"Hey, Falyn," her cousin, Jaxon, said, reaching down to give her a hug. Her eyes drifted over to the stunningly beautiful and incredibly stylish woman at his side. "Have you met my wife, Devine?"

"Please call me Dee," the beautiful woman said, pulling Falyn in for a hug, then holding her out at arm's length. "I've heard so much about you. Jaxon says your bed and breakfast is looking amazing!"

"It's coming together nicely," she replied. "You and Jaxon may need to come and stay. I know it's close to home, but the breakfast alone will be worth it."

"The triplets are 11 months old and on the move." Jaxon said, exhaustion in his eyes, as his gaze drifted down to his wife. "I think Dee and I could use a night away. What do you think, babe?"

"Yes, please," she said, cocking a coy brow at him.

Falyn smiled, happy for them, yet in her heart, the not fully healed wound of her recent betrayal still festered. Glancing around the group that was gathering, everyone was coupled up, and she wondered at that moment if she was going to be the only single person, other than Brooks and Georgie, of course. In her book, they didn't count. They were meant to be together, even if they hadn't realized it yet. Before that third-wheel feeling could fully settle in, Brooks and Georgie arrived, her brother and his life of the party energy distracting her from her thoughts.

Georgie walked straight up to her, gave her a hug and whispered in her ear, "I'm so glad you're here, Falyn. We singles need to stick together tonight."

The apprehension Falyn had been feeling moments earlier dwindled as she met Georgie's eyes, and suddenly didn't feel so alone. Georgie wrapped her arm around her as their group entered the bar. The driving beat of a country tune she didn't recognize filled the space as the crowded bar got fuller with their large group. She followed as they crossed the wooden dance floor to a large, reserved corner booth, an area that was large enough for their party. Falyn's gaze drifted around the entire bar, so much to take in. Dimly lit in ambiance, kitschy neon signs graced the open wall space, providing light along with the dance floor. Spotlights illuminated the long bar with a mirrored backdrop that occupied the opposite end of the room. *The place has its charms.* Not what she had gotten used to, but unquestionably a place the old Falyn would have frequented back in the day. *Let loose and have fun,* she told herself as she took in a deep breath and let it out slowly, steadying her remaining nerves.

The night carried on, their group taking to the dance floor and her dusting off some of her old moves. Before long she had to admit she was having fun. She had eased into conversation with Ever, Whitney and Dee and had a front-row seat to Brooks and Georgie flirting with their attraction for each other. *Nothing out of the ordinary there.* Falyn sipped the rest of her Coca-Cola, excused herself to the ladies at the table and slid out of the booth, dodging the patrons to get past the dance floor to the bar. Finding an open space on the side, she leaned onto the bar, patiently waiting for a bartender to notice her. She was reaching into her purse to pull out a twenty-dollar bill when she heard a deep, rich voice shout over the loud music, "What can I get you?"

Falyn looked up and her gaze met steely blue-grey eyes, intense and broody. The bartender's eyes softened as he unabashedly surveyed her, his gaze drifting back to meet hers. Heat rose up her neck to settle in her cheeks as her heart rate spiked and her mind went blank. *What the hell?* The handsome bartender chuckled lightly, the timbre of his voice deep and rich as he leaned onto the bar and placed his hand on hers. A sizzle of electrical current heated her skin, and her eyes flitted to his hand and back up to his remarkable eyes. "What would you like, Angel?" he asked again, a dashing smile curving his lips.

"Just...just a...Coke, please." She managed, internally groaning at how uncouth she was acting.

He nodded, scooping ice into a glass as he poured the cola, giving her a little side-eye. "I've never seen you around here. What's your name?"

Falyn hesitated as she examined him, quickly sizing him up. Everything about this man screamed bad boy. From the messy salt and pepper spikes of his perfectly disheveled hair to the black t-shirt that stretched over muscular shoulders and bulging biceps, to the sleeves of colorful tattoos that looked like a road map of hard living. Without question, he was not Falyn's type, and yet she couldn't help but admire how wildly attractive he was. Attractive and older, a whole lot older than her.

"I'm Falyn Isley. My brother is Brooks, the party in the

corner," she replied as he tossed a bar towel over his broad shoulder and casually leaned his colorful, ripped arms on the bar facing her.

"Ahh! The party from Primrose. Love that town, and Brooks is a great guy," he said, as his smoldering gaze pinned her. "I had no idea he had such a pretty sister," he added with a sly wink as he asked. "Are you from Primrose too?"

"I just moved back from Vancouver, but yes, I purchased the bed and breakfast on the outskirts of town." She replied, unsure why she was divulging all these details to a virtual stranger.

"A businesswoman. I like it," he said, his intense eyes laser-focused on her.

"I'm a chef actually, but yes," she replied, a blush starting to bloom on her cheeks from his stare. She looked away nervously, tucking her curls behind her ears and glanced at the twenty-dollar bill still in her hands.

"Your money's no good here, Angel. Your drinks are on me tonight," he said, putting out his hand to her. "I'm Sylvio Conti, the owner of this establishment."

She nodded, mouthing 'thank you' as she took his hand, that same sizzle and pop returning from the simple feel of his hand in hers. He lingered longer than would be considered simply friendly and smoothed his thumb over the soft skin between her thumb and index finger. The move was so slight, but it made her tremble. *Get yourself together, Falyn.* Reluctantly, she pulled her hand away and averted her gaze from the handsome bar owner and stepped away from the bar. As she walked away, she could feel his eyes follow her as she went.

* * *

SYLVIO'S EYES kept drifting over to the party in the corner of the bar. His eyeline of the strikingly beautiful woman, Falyn, being obstructed by patrons. *Man, she's beautiful. Petite, curvy in all the right places and those eyes... extraordinary.* Like pools of rich, dark, hot chocolate. Then there were those soft blonde curls that framed her beautiful face, which he itched to touch and slide his fingers through. *Were they as soft as they looked?* He had never considered himself to have a type, but if he did, it would be Falyn Isley. She wasn't like the other girls who came into the bar. She dressed and carried herself with an air of modesty and maturity that he liked. He was never into women that acted and dressed with the intention to draw attention to themselves. Maybe as the owner of The Pickled Pig he saw way more than his share of skin on a regular basis. He liked a woman with style, a little sophistication and his biggest turn on, intelligence. One brief meeting with Falyn and he could tell she was a young, intelligent woman, and so much more than she seemed. Just one look into those baby browns and he was certain he had met his match. A woman who was independent and could hold her own. *Sexy as hell.*

She also carried a little mystery behind her gorgeous gaze. When his eyes locked on hers, he was certain there was a story there, and he was intrigued. *How long has it been since a woman intrigued me like this?* Years certainly. In his 52 years he had done a lot of flirting, dated more than his share, and with his line of work, he met attractive women all the time. *But have I ever had such a visceral response to a woman before? Such an immediate attraction?* He wasn't sure if he had, at least not since his ex-wife.

Having been divorced for more than two decades, Sylvio seldom thought of that dark time in his life anymore. Having met his ex-wife Charity at the young age of 22, he was quickly enamored by the raven-haired beauty. Charity was young, vibrant, and free spirited and he loved her unbridled passion for life. She was like the sun in a dark room, and he could never get enough of that light.

Sylvio let out a pained breath and shook his head, trying to dispel the difficult memory. Picking up a bar rag, he spotted Falyn on the dance floor, her face bright and joyful, those gorgeous eyes sparkling under the dance floor spotlights. He leaned on the bar, watching her and wondering what her story was and if she would ever tell him.

CHAPTER 3

It was closing time, and Falyn glanced at the time on her watch: *2 a.m.* Not an uncommon hour for a chef. Everyone said their goodbyes in the parking lot, and she made her way to her car. The car was a loaner from her parents that they pulled out of the machine shed when she arrived back in Primrose. She wasn't about to complain, though. It got her from point A to point B and thus far was reliable enough that she didn't need to go car shopping.

Seeing the traffic jam to get out of the parking lot, she sat for a moment, reflecting on the fun of the night as she pulled out her phone. Swiping it open, she clicked on her camera app and swiped through the pictures she had taken, stopping on one of her and Brooks. She let out a little laugh at his big, goofy face. Having been close to her one and only sibling her entire life, she'd missed him terribly when she moved to Vancouver. Brooks managed to visit several times throughout the years, bringing his energy along with him, and she returned home to visit when she could, but it was hard not having him around. Another reason she was so happy to have returned to Primrose.

Glancing up from her phone, she set it down and noticed the parking lot was all but empty, only a few vehicles remaining. *How long was I swiping through my photos?* Slipping her key into the ignition, she turned it over, and it sputtered. *Seriously.* She tried several more times, and her car wouldn't fire up. Falyn groaned and rested her head on the steering wheel. *What options do I have? Tow truck, perhaps? Call a friend, but who?* She wasn't close enough to anyone in town that she could simply call them in the middle of the night. Besides, everyone she knew well enough to call had been at the bar tonight and on their way home. Her parents would never wake up at this hour. Brooks was a no-go as he was bringing Georgie home and she had partaken in more than her share of birthday libations. *What should I do?*

The loud rumble of a motorcycle broke her from her thoughts, and her head popped up, startled at the sound. Headlights appeared from behind the building, approaching her vehicle as she quickly flipped the locks and tried to look calm. A classic Harley Davidson pulled up beside her, and she couldn't make out the silhouette on the bike. Her heart pounded outside her chest as the man on the bike removed his helmet. It was Sylvio, the handsome silver fox bartender, and although he was essentially a stranger, something about it being him gave her a sense of calm and relief. He cut the engine of his bike, climbed off, his dark jeans stretching over muscular thighs, a black leather jacket squaring his shoulders and making him look like a bad-boy fantasy. He knocked gently on her driver's side window and stepped back, allowing Falyn to climb out of her vehicle. Standing in front of her, he was tall, Falyn guessed at least six foot two inches, and his broad muscular shoulders, chest and arms gave him an imposing stature with or without his worn leather jacket. She let her eyes drift up his rather impressive upper body and meet his handsome smile and twinkling blue-grey eyes that crinkled endearingly at the edges.

"Hi," he said simply, the low timbre of his voice oddly soothing.

"Hi," she replied softly as she swallowed nervously, unable to divert her gaze from his.

"Are you having some car trouble?" he asked, glancing over to her sad sack of a sedan.

Falyn scrunched up her nose and followed his gaze. Time to take off the rose-colored glasses; her loaner car had seen better days. She sighed, "Yeah, it won't turn over."

"Do you mind if I take a look?" he asked, gesturing to the hood of the car.

Falyn shook her head and gestured to the vehicle, offering him a grateful smile. Opening her driver's side door, she popped the hood with Sylvio there to unlatch and prop it up. Rounding her vehicle, she joined him as he leaned in and reached inside. She stood beside him, watching but not really registering what he was doing. She knew nothing about vehicles, and while living in

Vancouver never felt the need to own one. There had been no need when there was public transportation, and later, when she and Pierre were a couple, Uber, taxis and hired drivers on special occasions met their necessities.

Sylvio rose to his full height and winced. "I think you have a dead battery here," he said, pulling out a bandana from his pocket and wiping his hands on it. "I know a guy who can replace it for you, but it won't happen tonight. Let me call a tow truck for you." Sylvio pulled out his phone and dialed a number before Falyn had a chance to register what he was doing and give her obligatory protest. *I'm fully capable of calling a tow truck myself.* But before she could open her mouth, Sylvio was talking with someone and with just a handful of words exchanged, ended the call and turned to face her. "He's sending over a tow truck, and they'll get it up and running for you first thing on Monday morning," he said, sliding his phone into the inside pocket of his jacket. "Do you have backup transportation until then?"

"I'll manage." She answered, wrapping her arms around herself, giving into a shiver, and cursing herself for not grabbing a jacket when she left home. The spring night was cold and damp as they stood, just the two of them, in the now abandoned parking lot. Sylvio's brows drew together in concern as he proceeded to slip out of his leather jacket.

"What are you doing?" she asked as she watched him remove his jacket and come behind her, sitting it on her shoulders. The gesture was sweet and chivalrous.

"You're cold and I wouldn't be a gentleman if I didn't

offer you my jacket," he replied, his colorfully tattooed arms now exposed to the elements.

Falyn glanced up at him, slipped her arms into the two long sleeves, and wrapped her arms around herself, feeling instantly warmer as the smell of leather, citrus, and cedar surrounded her. *His scent.* She covertly inhaled the intoxicating smell as her eyes raked over his exposed arms. The colorful ink that covered them was intriguing to her and made her want to reach out and touch them, just to make sure they were real.

"You don't look like a gentleman." She replied, letting her eyes meet his and cocking a curious eyebrow at him.

"Looks can be deceiving," he replied, his eyes sparkling with mirth.

A smile tugged at Falyn's lips as she added. "The Harley, the leather jacket, the ink, how's a girl to know? What I see is a stereotypical bad boy."

A low, growly laugh rumbled from Sylvio's chest, and his steely eyes flashed with humor as they crinkled. "You, Falyn, are not only beautiful but feisty."

* * *

SYLVIO STARED DOWN AT FALYN, her big beautiful brown eyes mirroring the mischief of his own, and he liked it. He liked it a lot. What she lacked in stature, she made up for in personality, and something told him she could dish it out as good as she could take it.

The bright lights of a tow truck turned onto the parking lot, breaking them from their stare, and Falyn stepped back from Sylvio, his arms itching to draw her closer rather than have further distance between them. The tow truck parked in front of both her car and his bike. The driver, a young man dressed in coveralls with the name Eric embroidered on the lapel and wearing a cap with the logo of the towing company, jumped out of the cab, the sound of his steel-toe boots heavy on the pavement.

"What do we have here?" he asked cockily, with an amused look on his face as he looked between the car, Sylvio, and let his eyes linger uncomfortably long on Falyn. A wicked smile of appreciation curled the edge of his lips as he unapologetically looked Falyn up and down.

Who does this kid think he is? Sylvio didn't like that look so protectively he stepped in behind Falyn so close her jasmine perfume caught on the early morning breeze, almost derailing the intention of his show of dominance. Sylvio narrowed his gaze, pinning young Eric with the evil eye. Eric, catching his "back off" look, immediately cleared his throat and painted a serious expression on his face as he stepped towards the car. *Smart kid.*

He leaned in, his head disappearing under the hood, and a moment later, he emerged and confirmed what Sylvio thought was the problem. "Definitely the battery. I'll tow it back to the shop, and we'll get to it first thing next week. Let me go get a form for you to fill out so we have your information."

As the young man turned to go back to his truck, Falyn glanced up at Sylvio over her shoulder and with an amused glint in her eye, she said, "You just intimidated that kid."

"I put him in his place," he replied. "He needs to learn not to leer at women that way. Especially a woman in distress."

"A woman in distress," she echoed with a dubious guffaw as she turned to face him and crossed her arms over her chest. "Do you think that's what I am, some weak damsel in distress that can't figure out how to get my car to a mechanic shop on my own?"

"No, I never said that," he replied, a little surprised and rather turned on by her assertive confrontation. "I have no question that you could figure this out on your own. In fact, I'm pretty sure you could tell that punk to take a hike or kick him in the balls if he tried something, but kids like that need to understand what's appropriate and what's not. Looking at you like a piece of meat is not."

"And you don't look at women that way, Mr. Bartender?" she countered with a sardonic tone.

He stepped closer, so close she needed to crane her neck to meet his gaze. "I wouldn't be a hot-blooded man if I didn't appreciate a beautiful woman," he replied, bringing his hand up to finger one of her curls that framed her face, his fingers ever so slightly brushing the side of her cheek. Falyn's eyes fluttered, her breath noticeably hitching, although never giving up her ground with her fiery stare. "Despite my chosen profession, Ms. Isley, I respect women. Some may even say I worship them."

Visibly flustered by his comment, Falyn raised her chin and squared her shoulders, taking on a challenging stance.

Damn this woman. Why does she have to be so incredibly sexy? An amused smile curled his lips as the tow truck driver returned with a clipboard, interrupting their banter. Falyn signed the necessary forms, and they watched as the tow truck driver hooked up her car and drove off the parking lot, taillights disappearing into the night.

They stood there a moment, a quiet falling between them until Falyn broke the silence. "I guess I need to call a cab or Uber."

"No Uber in St. Augustine, and a cab all the way back to Primrose is going to cost a fortune," Sylvio replied. "Let me give you a ride home."

"On that death trap?" she replied with an incredulous guffaw, gesturing to his bike and shaking her head. "Not a chance."

Sylvio shook his head as a deep chuckle rumbled from his chest. He walked over to his bike, unclipped a spare helmet from the seat and strode over to her, meeting her defiant gaze. "I've been driving a Harley for over half my life and never once have I gotten into an accident. If there is anyone that can get you to Primrose safely, it's me," he said, handing her the helmet as he confidently strode back to his bike and mounted it. Glancing over to her, Falyn's face was a mix of uncertainty and distrust as she stared at the helmet in her hands. A look he wanted to explore deeper. But for now, it was late, and he needed to get her home. "C'mon, Falyn. Get on the fucking bike." She glared back at him, her eyes flashing with stubborn defiance for a moment, then letting out an exasperated growl, she conceded, putting on the helmet and struggling with the strap.

"Come here," he calmly demanded, gesturing for her to

come closer. She hesitantly obliged, her brown eyes wide with trepidation and frustration. He reached over gently, tucking stray curls into the helmet and locking his gaze on hers as he snapped the strap in place and tightened it so it was secure under her chin. "Too tight?" he asked, searching her wary gaze. She simply shook her head, and he smiled, tipping her chin to meet his eyes. "I promise I'll get you home safely."

What on earth am I doing? Falyn climbed onto Sylvio's Harley Davidson, her thighs circling his narrow hips and wrapping around his muscular jean-clad legs, resting her feet on the passenger pegs. He slipped on his helmet, fastening it as she straightened out his jacket, a leather hug around her body, and he turned his head, catching her in his peripheral vision. "Make sure to hold on tight, okay? Squeeze your thighs and wrap your arms around my waist." She awkwardly slid her arms around his torso, barely long enough to make it fully around, and she locked her fingers over his taut, rippled stomach. A six-pack. *Seriously.* She internally moaned, his lean and strong torso twitching under her touch, every part of him solid as a rock. The awareness of their proximity made her traitorous body surge with her awakening libido. His manly scent enveloped her, and she took a self-indulgent inhale into his shoulder, letting the scent swirl her head and rouse her senses. Sylvio started the bike, the loud rumble vibrating through her thighs squeezing into his hips, sending her pulse and arousal into overdrive. "Ready?" he asked over the growl of the bike.

"Yes," she replied, gripping him tighter as the bike kicked forward and then eased off the parking lot onto the main highway. The cool wind whipped around Falyn's face, and she rested her cheek on his back. The smell of the pavement, his cologne and leather of the jacket provided comfort as adrenaline pumped through her body.

The bar on the outskirts of St. Augustine faded from sight as Sylvio took to the edge of the small city, avoiding the downtown, and before she knew it, they were on the highway headed in the direction of Primrose. Her hands finding their purchase, his muscles straining as he controlled the bike. She glanced around his broad shoulders to see his strong, colorfully tattooed arms bulging, veins popping as he gripped the handlebars. A man in complete control of his motorcycle. Falyn relaxed against him, her grip on his torso still firm but the tension and nervousness diminishing as she molded against his body. There was something about the way it felt being this close, her safety in the hands of a virtual stranger, and yet, uncharacteristically in this moment on the back of his bike, she trusted him. She felt safe. Sighing against his back, she could feel him slow down. The sign for Primrose passed them by as she looked up, the streetlights of Main Street illuminating the night. He cruised past the various businesses, past the Eazy Café, towards the north end of town. Slowing down at the sign for Prairie Charm Bed and Breakfast and turning onto the driveway, he pulled up next to the cottage and cut the engine of the bike. They sat there a moment, her still wrapped around him securely, trying to steady her racing heart.

"Are you okay, Angel?" he asked, his voice low and gravely as his large hand rested on hers, still holding onto him.

"Yeah," she breathed out against his back. "That was my first ride on a motorcycle, and don't get an inflated ego by me saying this, but it was exhilarating." Sylvio laughed deeply, the muscles of his stomach rippling with the shake of his body.

With trembling hands, Falyn removed the helmet, freeing her curls, and carefully climbed off the bike. Her thighs still vibrated from the engine, causing her to wobble a little. Sylvio caught her, his strong hands on her waist under his jacket as he steadied her. The heat of his hands burned through the thin fabric of her blouse, as his thumbs found the skin just under the hem and past the waist of her jeans. He caressed the skin softly, causing a shiver to roll through her, her skin immediately turning hot. His magnificent eyes twinkled in the porch light, and her breath caught as the tip of her tongue darted out to wet her bottom lip. Sylvio tracked her tongue and with a low growl, he pulled her closer, his hands circling her waist and her hands splayed on his chest. He was still straddling his bike, and she wasn't sure what came over her, but she climbed back on, facing him, her legs hooking over his thick thighs, their cores mere inches apart. *Who is this brazen woman?*

Maybe it was the adrenaline of the ride. Maybe it was the feel of his warm hands ever so slightly caressing her bare skin. Or perhaps it was the way the light hit the handsome angles of his chiseled face, or the way the moon glinted in his incredible eyes, but Falyn wanted to kiss Sylvio. A deep desperation to be thoroughly and wantonly kissed overtook her mind and body.

"I need you to kiss me," she confessed, her heart beating wildly in her chest.

He sucked in a hissing breath through his teeth as a low, rumbly growl escaped his throat. "Angel, if I kiss you, I'm not sure I'm going to be able to stop," he said, his hands sliding over the globes of her ass, pulling impossibly closer. "I'm going to want to kiss, here." he said, taking her face between his hands and planting a warm wet kiss on her cheek. "And here," he said, planting another on the side of her neck, the scruff of his chin, causing goosebumps to pebble her skin as his eyes met hers. "And I'm going to want to kiss down your body, exploring every inch of your gorgeous skin."

"Maybe I want that." She replied, her voice breathy. "Maybe I need your hands on me."

* * *

AN OPEN INVITATION TO take her inside and have his way with her lingered in the hot and steamy air between them. It had been a long time since someone tempted him like this. Made him want to get out of his head and simply take what he wanted. What she was willingly offering. Making him want to forget the past and live in the here and now. *What was it about this woman?* There were the obvious reasons he was attracted to her. Her striking beauty and sexy petite body with succulent curves. The challenging looks she gave him, her guard up high, the mystery in her gaze. Her feistiness and smart mouth. *Fuck, that sexy mouth.* His eyes darted to her tantalizing pink lips, parted ever so slightly. He hardly knew her, but he wanted to know so much more. There was something indescribable. An intensity between them.

Sylvio's lips curled up into a cunning smile as he said, "I'll kiss you on one condition."

"What's that?" she asked, searching his face.

"You go out on a date with me," he challenged. "I'm not a one-night stand kind of guy."

"Really, is that what you think I want?" she volleyed.

"I think at this moment, yes you do. While the adrenaline of being on the back of my bike and the thrill of wrapping yourself around me is pumping through your body," he replied, meeting her lustful eyes with honesty. "I think you would regret it in the morning, though. I don't want to be a regret."

Falyn searched his eyes, the desire there softening into a blooming smile. *She has the prettiest smile.* "You really are a gentleman, aren't you?"

"I told you I was," he replied, her eyes searching for the truth and softening when she found her answer. "Will you let me take you out?" he asked again, his eyes drifting to her rosy lips, wanting to kiss her more with each passing second.

"Yes, Sylvio. I'll go out with you," she replied with a smile, as she brought the corner of her lip between her teeth and met his intense gaze.

Sylvio reached up, cupping her face in his large hands, his fingers threading through her lush curls as he drew her closer, her eyes fluttering closed as he claimed her lips, gently at first then deepening as she opened allowing his tongue to taste and explore. Her lips were soft and supple, as pillowy and perfect as he imagined they would be. She kissed him back, giving as much as she was taking, and for a moment, he doubted his choice to keep tonight to just this single kiss. Falyn matched each brush of his lips and sweep of his tongue, and he was sure this was the best kiss of his life. She ran her hands up his arms, her fingers gripping the bulge of his biceps, then sliding up his arms, over his shoulders and into his hair. He groaned against her lips as she wove her fingers into his hair and tugged gently, pressing him forward, deepening their kiss. His arousal strained painfully against the fly of his jeans, beginning its own protest. Mid-kiss, he pulled away, a small whimper escaping Falyn's throat. Her pretty lips were bitten with their bruising kiss, their breaths coming out quick and labored.

"I'm going to call you," he said, enveloping her in a hug. Her body exhaled in his embrace as she wrapped her arms around him, and her hands splayed on his back. Falyn hesitantly pulled away, shimmying his leather jacket off her shoulders and offering it to him. He slipped it on, and she grinned, pulling up his collar to make it stand up, before she grabbed both sides of his collar and brought him in for another chaste but scorching kiss.

Releasing their embrace, she let out a conceding breath before carefully unraveling herself from him, climbing off the bike and landing on her two feet beside it. Turning, she faced him, the glow of the porch light making the crown of her dark blonde curls glow like the halo of an angel. *My angel.* He put his helmet back on and fired up the engine of his bike as she turned and slowly walked towards the front door of her cottage. Turning to do a double take, she flashed him that gorgeous smile as he revved the engine of the bike and kicked up gravel as he turned around and sped down the driveway into the prairie night.

CHAPTER 4

Falyn woke Sunday morning, her warm comforter wrapped around her like a cocoon. As soon as her head hit her pillow, she was out, her night filled with dreams of mesmerizing blue-grey eyes and strong tattooed arms holding her against a rock-hard chest. She reached up and touched her lips, remembering that mind-melting kiss on his bike, how good his soft hair felt in her grip, and how impossibly sexy the scratch of his facial scruff felt against the soft skin of her neck. She had never been sexually inhibited, but even she had surprised herself. How she boldly straddled him, the vibration of his bike still pulsing through her core. *What did he think of that?* Obviously, he liked it. She couldn't help but notice the straining bulge in his jeans and the way he gripped her ass, drawing her closer. *That was so damn hot. He was so damn hot. Since when did she have something for much older, tattooed, Harley-driving bad boys?* She had always dated men who were clean-cut, stylish, and she had always had a bit of a thing for a power suit. Sylvio was not a suit kind of guy; she was sure of that. *Since when am I into tight t-shirts and jeans stretched over bulging thigh muscles and a taut butt? And grey hair? Why was it so sexy? Sylvio is evidently older than me, but by how much?* She wasn't opposed to age gaps in couples. She and Pierre had a seven-year age difference. She had seen it work with Georgie's parents, Patrick and Emmaline Donahue, who were 20 years apart in age. But she had never considered getting involved with a silver fox herself. Sylvio Conti was the definition of a silver fox. A very fit, very sexy man in his 50s?

Falyn shook her head. None of that mattered. What mattered was if she was ready for this. It had been a year and a half since she and Pierre split and nine months since her divorce was finalized. He had moved on thoroughly, having welcomed a child and apparently now engaged to his mistress. Didn't she deserve to at the very least date? *Of course, you do.*

Falyn picked up her phone from her nightstand. Swiping it open, what seemed like a million notifications popped up on screen. She sifted through them one by one. A text from her mom, asking if she would come Tuesday night for dinner to celebrate Brooks' birthday, countless emails from contractors, and an email confirmation from the mechanic shop regarding her car. Among them all was a text from an unknown number. The text read:

Good morning, Angel. This is Sylvio. I can neither confirm nor deny that I saw your number on the form you filled out for the tow truck driver and memorized it. One of my hidden talents. Call me when you get this. I don't mind texting, but I would rather hear your beautiful voice.

Falyn smiled, unraveling herself from her comforter and swinging her legs out of bed. She sat there a moment, getting her bearings as she re-read his text and closed her phone, making her way to the bathroom to take care of her morning needs. She washed her hands and face before exiting the bathroom and entering her tiny kitchen. The cottage kitchen was a pocket of space compared to the large kitchen in the guest house, but Falyn prided herself on making anything work. Reaching into her refrigerator, she pulled out fresh berries and yogurt, and searching through the cupboard she pulled out a pouch of organic granola and some protein powder. Making quick work of fixing herself a power bowl, she started a pot of coffee and as she watched it brew, she glanced back at her phone sitting on the little butcher block island. Leaning against the counter and taking a heaping spoonful of her breakfast into her mouth, she stared at her phone, willing it to ring. She wanted him to call. She wanted to call him. If she were being honest, she was itching to. *But what if last night was a one-off? What if he, in the light of day, reconsidered her? Let's face it, everyone was more attractive after a night of partying. He did text you this morning, though. That doesn't sound like a man not interested.* Appeasing her inner voice, she quickly picked up her phone and started to text.

* * *

SYLVIO REACHED for the coffeepot and poured himself another mug full. He loved lazy Sundays. The Pickled Pig was closed, and although he usually spent the afternoon there, sifting through paperwork and making the necessary orders for the week, today he was choosing to laze around in nothing but flannel pajama pants while watching Netflix. His phone buzzed against the counter, and he picked it up quickly, hoping it was a certain young blonde, brown-eyed beauty from last night. A slow smile curved his lips as her name popped up, and he eagerly swiped open his phone reading:

Good morning handsome, or should I call you silver fox? Hmmm...I haven't decided yet.

He laughed, the slow, gravelly rumble of it coming from deep in his chest. He liked this woman. All sassy and smart and so goddamn beautiful it was blinding. He was never one to chase after what the world seemed to deem conventionally beautiful women. The tall, model-like, svelte women in tiny dresses with long, straightened hair and far too polished makeup. Women who looked like they had just done an online makeup tutorial, perfectly primped and glossy. They were not his thing. He liked a woman who was unique, didn't look cookie-cutter but was beautiful in a natural way. Give him a woman with her hair wild or messily pulled up at the top of her head, no makeup, and if there was even a hint of freckles, he was a sold man. Charity had freckles. A smattering of tiny brown dots dappled the bridge of her nose. God, he loved those freckles, even if she hated them. Sometimes when she was asleep, he would count them. 23 gorgeous spots, the same number of years she was when she died. He shook his head, trying to dispel the awful memory.

Reaching again for his phone, he dialed Falyn's number.

"Hi," she answered, the slight rasp in her voice both endearing and sexy.

"Hi," he replied. "How did you sleep?"

"Like a baby," she answered. "And you?"

"After a cold shower, I slept," he replied honestly. Flashing back to how she'd straddled him, the heat of her body pressed against his and the taste of her sensual lips and tongue, matching him brush for brush and stroke for stroke. "You got me a little worked up, Angel."

"I noticed. Those tight pants you wear don't exactly leave much to imagination." She chuckled, the sound of her laugh rich, bright, and womanly. A sound that made his heart beat faster.

"Were you checking out the package?" he asked coyly.

"No, but I was appreciating it." She volleyed with facetiousness in her tone.

Sylvio laughed. As suspected, he had met his match with this woman, and he was truly enjoying this tit for tat. "Other than your deep appreciation for my tight jeans, what are some other things you like?"

"Are you asking if I like bouquets of red roses and long walks on the beach?" She asked cheekily.

"If that's part of the list, then yes." He replied with a chuckle. "Tell me more about you."

* * *

FALYN WASN'T sure where to begin or how much to share. She liked Sylvio, was enjoying this conversation, and wanted to know more about him as well. But, with take there had to be give, and she needed to be honest about her past and put herself out there. If he didn't like it, then she'd live with the memory of that passionate kiss on his bike and move on.

"Well, I'm a native Primrosian, as you already know. I moved back home about six months ago after spending over ten years in Vancouver," she replied.

"What brought you to the West Coast?"

"Culinary school at first, and then I met my ex-husband and ended up staying." She replied, pausing to hear his reaction.

"Ex-husband. Are you separated, divorced, or still figuring it out?" he asked with a hint of wariness in his tone.

"Nothing to figure out. Pierre cheated multiple times, and his last mistress ended up pregnant, so we're good and divorced now." She replied so matter-of-factly that she shocked herself. The line fell silent, and Falyn bit her lip nervously, wondering if her honest and blunt answer had divulged too much. "Sylvio, are you still there?"

"Do you mind if I come over?" he asked.

"Now?"

"Yes, I can be there in 30 minutes."

"Sylvio, I..." she was about to protest, but he cut her off.

"Be there soon."

* * *

PULLING into the driveway of Prairie Charm Bed and Breakfast, Sylvio parked his bike on the side of the cottage and cut the engine. As soon as Falyn told him about her divorce, the need to see her overwhelmed him. Despite the matter-of-fact way she shared about the demise of her marriage, he could hear the emotion hovering on the edges of her words. He too understood the pain of infidelity all too well.

Climbing off his bike, he slung a leather pack across his body and stuffed his keys into the pocket of his leather jacket. Rounding the house, Falyn was already there on the stoop, her dark blonde curls swept up in a messy bun at the top of head, with ringlets escaping haphazardly. Her face was makeup-free, tiny freckles sprinkled across her nose and the tops of her cheeks, and her brown eyes were big and beautiful as they sparkled in the midday sun. Dressed in black leggings, a V-neck lilac t-shirt that dipped low to show off the swells of her breasts and a long, soft-looking cream-colored cardigan, he smiled at how impossibly gorgeous she looked. His eyes drifted down to her bare feet, so dainty and prettily painted with lilac nail polish, and all he could think was, *she's perfect.*

"Hey there, Angel," he said, walking up to her. A smile grew on her face as he approached.

"Couldn't stay away from me?" she asked, cocking a curious brow at him.

"More like I didn't want to," he volleyed as he enveloped her in a hug.

She tensed at first, then her shoulders eased as she buried her head in his chest, and he found the softness of her neck, his fingertips caressing gently over the exposed skin. She inhaled deeply and let out a breath slowly as he held her. They stood there for a long moment, and when she pulled away, her face was flushed, and her eyes glistened with unshed tears.

"You sounded like you needed a friend," he said, his hand coming up and fingering the loose curls framing her face.

"Is that what we are? Friends?" she asked, meeting his gaze.

"It's a nice place to start, don't you think?" Sylvio asked, offering her a smile.

Falyn's smile mirrored his, and he could see the relief in her eyes as she answered, "It's a perfect place to start."

WELCOMING Sylvio into her little cottage, he removed his leather crossbody bag and slid out of his leather jacket, hanging it on an open hook by the door. Now in the light of day, Falyn could truly check him out and admire not only his handsome face but his unbelievable body. Sylvio's greying hair was shaved short on the sides, longer on top, which was now sexily disheveled by his helmet. His jawline, square and strong, and dusted with salt and pepper scruff that she found very attractive. His eyes were the most striking shade, blue with flecks of silver that crinkled endearingly with smile lines at the sides when he was amused. Clad in a tight grey t-shirt with a Harley Davidson logo stretched across his rather impressive pecs and tight black jeans that hugged his thick thighs and tight butt just right, Sylvio Conti was an impressive specimen of a man by all accounts and Falyn didn't mind the view.

"Make yourself at home," she said, gesturing to the stools set on the other side of the small island in her kitchen.

Sylvio took a seat as she rounded the island and continued her meal prep, cutting a green apple into quarters, coring it and making thin, precise slices.

"What are you making?" he asked, curiously leaning over the counter.

"Croque Monsieur," she replied. "It's basically a thick-cut ham and Swiss sandwich lathered in mayonnaise and more cheese and baked until toasted and melty. I add the green apple for a little extra twist."

"Sounds fancy and delicious," he replied. "Don't think I've ever tried it before."

"It was something I would make when my ex and I were both home," she replied, letting out a sigh as she set three sandwiches on a baking sheet and popped them into the oven.

"How long were you married?" Sylvio asked curiously.

"Seven years, not including the nine months that it took to finalize our divorce," she replied, meeting his gaze.

"You must have been young when you met him then."

"Just turned 22, fresh out of culinary school and a naïve country girl swept up into big-city life," she replied.

"So, you're 32 now, then," Sylvio inquired.

She nodded and cocked an eyebrow at him. "And you are?"

"52."

"20 years my senior," she replied, a slow smile creeping up her face.

"Does that bother you?" he countered, leaning forward, his strong, colorful forearms resting on the countertop.

"No," she replied, mirroring him by leaning her elbows on the counter and capturing his stare. "I've never given much thought to age, to be honest. It's really just a number."

"Good," he replied, inching his fingers forward to touch hers as he took her hand and smoothed his thumb over the soft skin between her thumb and pointer finger, just like he had done the night before. That unmistakable sizzle was back, surging and strong.

"So, have you been married before?" she asked curiously. "Or are you a career bachelor?"

He chuckled deeply as he answered. "Yes, 25 years ago. She was unfaithful, and that ultimately ended our marriage." Sylvio glanced down at their touching hands, tracing light little circles over her palm. Now when his eyes came up, he met her gaze; despair and what looked like guilt flashed in his eyes. *Guilt. What did he have to be guilty about when his ex-wife was the one who was unfaithful?* Falyn had a feeling there was more to the story.

TALKING about his past was never easy. But he wasn't about to lay out all his cards right away with Falyn. His ex, Charity, had been unfaithful, and that was all she needed to know for now. Even just talking about it made the guilt rise to the surface like an incoming wave threatening to drown him. Despite the rush of complex feelings thinking about his past brought on, Sylvio wanted Falyn to know she wasn't alone, and that being betrayed by someone you loved was not something easy to overcome.

The oven timer beeped, breaking them from their conversation, and Falyn slipped on oven mitts and opened the oven. The most glorious smell of baked sharp cheese and rich ham filled the kitchen, and Sylvio's stomach growled.

"Hungry?" Falyn asked, mirth flashing in her beautiful brown eyes.

"Starved," he replied, rubbing his hands together as he watched her lift a sandwich off the baking sheet onto a plate, then cut it diagonally.

"Be careful, the cheese will be hot," she said, sliding the plate over to him and proceeding to plate one for herself. "Do you want to join me on the couch? Sundays right now are for indulgent food and movies, at least for the next few weeks."

"What's coming in the next few weeks?" he asked, grabbing both of their plates as she filled two glasses with iced tea and led him over to the plush couch in the small living room.

"The Grand Opening Weekend for the bed and breakfast." She replied. "I'm excited, but scared as well."

"Understandable. Opening a business is always anxiety-producing, but it's rewarding too. I remember when I opened my first business, I was 23 years old and didn't have a clue what I was doing."

"So, you haven't always been the beloved bar owner of The Pickled Pig?" she asked, curling her legs up and tucking them as she balanced her plate.

"No, my first business was a custom bike shop, actually," he replied.

"That tracks," Falyn answered with a wink. "So why then jump from that to a bar?"

"I wanted a place where people could gather, listen to good music and unwind. Also, self-indulgently I wanted to own a bar like the one in the movie *Roadhouse*," he said with a laugh and a shrug.

"Like that old Patrick Swayze movie?" she asked, amusement in her tone.

"Yep. Still a favorite of mine," he replied, glancing at the sandwich on his plate. "Is it safe to dig in?"

She nodded, watching as he picked up half of the sandwich and bit into it. His eyes widened with appreciation as he chewed and nodded his head. Swallowing, he said, "Angel, this may be the best damn sandwich I've ever eaten. Seriously, if the food at your bed and breakfast is half this good, book me every weekend."

* * *

FALYN WATCHED Sylvio from the corner of her eye, taking in his reactions as they watched *Roadhouse* together. After a brief description, Falyn agreed to watch it and she had to admit it was pretty good. But what was even better was watching Sylvio watch his favorite movie. The man was seriously cute, eagerly anticipating the scenes he knew so well: How he smiled at his favorite parts, let out a low, rumbly chuckle from deep in his chest when he found something funny, and how his strong, muscular arms tensed during the fight scenes. This unexpected crasher of her quiet Sunday provided her with much-needed entertainment and companionship. It was not lost on Falyn how comfortable she felt around him. Sylvio carried with him a calming presence that she hadn't experienced before with a man.

She smiled, her elbow resting on the side of the couch, her fingers twirling the springy curls that escaped her updo. Sylvio glanced over at her, a slow, sly smile curling his lips as he reached for her feet and pulled them onto his lap, making her shift onto her backside to face him.

"You have the prettiest feet," he said, sliding his rough hands over the tops of them and down the underside, making her squirm. "Ticklish?"

"A little," she answered, meeting his gaze.

"Good to know," he said, as he applied pressure to the sole of her feet with his thumb and slid it up the length to her toes. An unexpected deep, throaty moan escaped, and her pulse quickened as he did it again, this time sliding his fingers between her toes. Sylvio grinned at her wickedly as he continued to rub her feet with expertise, finding each pressure point and one delicious spot that made her pulse between her legs. "Feel good?"

"So good," she breathed out, meeting his gaze, her eyes half-lidded with contented pleasure. "Where did you learn to do this?"

"Riding a motorcycle has its additional benefits. Strong hands are one of them," he replied, the tip of his tongue peeking out to moisten his lips.

Falyn's eyes followed that movement, zoning in on the wetness of his perfect lips with the memory of their scorching kiss on his bike last night jumbling her thoughts and making her pulse quicken. She wanted to kiss him again. Desperately. The desire to feel that hot tongue slide against hers, overwhelming. Her lips parted slightly, and her breaths came out labored. *Am I panting?* The realization of what this man was doing to her, almost too much yet not enough, caused Falyn to make a split-second decision to take what she wanted. Pulling her feet away, he met her gaze, now burning with desire, and his eyes darkened, mirroring hers. She shifted off the couch and climbed onto his lap to straddle his thighs.

"What are you doing, Angel?" he asked gruffly, desire edging his deep voice.

"Taking what I want," she replied, rocking her core over the rock-hard bulge pressing against the fly of his jeans. Sylvio threw his head back against the couch, and she lowered her lips to his adams apple, circling it with her warm wet tongue as she kissed a trail over the column of his strained neck. Hands coming up, she threaded her fingers into his hair and pulled his mouth to hers. Capturing his lips, she pressed her peaked breasts into his hard chest, her pelvis gyrating in slow sensual circles over his arousal. They kissed, equally matched, hard, intense, mind-melding. Their mouths opened, inviting each other's tongues to tangle, drawing each other in deeper. He tasted sweet and savory; his lips so brilliantly firm yet deliciously soft. No one, not even Pierre, had kissed her like this. Deep, sensual, wildly passionate, yet in full control. Sylvio's large hands cupped her behind, pressing her core into his as she unapologetically rubbed against him, finding friction through the thin layers of her leggings and underwear. Soaked with arousal, her bundle of nerves throbbing, needing more, she pulled at his t-shirt, finding the hem and clawing it up his body. He took over, lifting it over his head, as she helped him out of it and threw it to the floor. Pulling her lips away from his, she took in the exquisite, hard, rippling edges of his upper body, and her mouth salivated, wanting to lick every angle and trace every line of his tattoos. She was never particularly attracted to tattooed men, but the colorful tapestry on his body was breathtaking, and she wanted to map each one. Slipping off her cardigan and reaching for the hem of her shirt, he slowly lifted it, exposing the supple skin at her waist as he peeled it past her breasts and over her head. Her white lace bra left little to the imagination, and his eyes dilated as they feasted on her curves.

"Fuck, you're gorgeous," he growled out as he pulled her towards him, crashing their lips together again in a scintillating kiss.

SYLVIO DIDN'T KNOW what he wanted to kiss, touch or explore first, but one look at the swells of Falyn's tantalizing breasts and his mouth watered to taste them. Letting his lips roam down the column of her neck, he slid his hands up the sides of her waist to the underside of her full breasts, cupping them and teasing her rigid peaks with his thumbs through the thin lace of her bra. His lips trailed down to her throat, to the hollow there, an unexpected erogenous zone as he dipped his tongue into it before he kissed his way down to the swells of her perfect curves.

"Take my bra off," she rasped, her voice wanton with need. Reaching around her back, he unfastened it, letting it fall away, leaving her writhing topless on his lap.

He had always had an appreciation for the curves of a woman. Full hips, a rounded ass, but breasts... breasts were without question his kryptonite. And Falyn had perfect breasts. Not too big, not too small, the perfect handful, with pebbled rosy nipples that tilted upright, begging for his mouth to suckle them. Drawing a pebbled peak into his mouth, he wrapped his lips around the nub and teased it with his tongue. Falyn threw her head back, a loud moan escaping her lips as she rocked harder over his strained jeans. He sucked her in, and she gasped as she ground hard over him, her head coming up and her gaze meeting his. Her lust-filled eyes clouded over and her breath caught on a gasp as she shook, her entire body trembling as her orgasm took over. Her thighs vibrated as his hands gripped her hips and he pressed her core to his, supporting her body. Her gyrations slowed, and she came down from the high, her body flushing with heat and settling in her cheeks.

He released her nipple with a pop, and she collapsed against his chest, her head buried in his neck. Sylvio ran his hands over her bare back, and up over her neck, caressing the base of her scalp and trailing back down again. They sat like that for a long time, her hot breath at his neck, her soft breasts pressed into his hard chest, his hands gently caressing her smooth back. Sylvio hadn't found his release, but having witnessed hers was not only beautiful but unspeakably erotic.

She shivered in his hold, and he wrapped her in his arms, holding her against the heat of his body. *Everything about this woman is special.* An innate protectiveness filled his chest as he thought about how another man could cheat on her and make her feel like she wasn't enough for him. *Who could take a woman like Falyn for granted? I would never. If Falyn were mine, I would hold on tight to her and never let her go.*

CHAPTER 5

The next few weeks flew by, and Prairie Charm Bed and Breakfast's grand opening was fast approaching. To celebrate the grand opening, Falyn prepared a special Sunday Brunch, which would be open for the bed and breakfast guests and then a later morning service by invitation only. On the guest list: her family, closest friends, those that helped with the renovation, and of course, Sylvio.

Sylvio. Just thinking about the handsome man made her hot and bothered. His literal work of art body, chiseled and tattooed to bad-boy perfection. Those insanely beautiful blue-grey eyes, so intense and smoldering. Sylvio was the epitome of a silver fox, and she was here for it. However, beyond his sexy outward persona was a smart, insightful man who was funny and kind and cared deeply for others. And perhaps that was even sexier than his sinfully good looks.

It had been weeks since their Sunday afternoon together, both busy and consumed with their businesses.

Regardless, at the end of every day, Sylvio called, and in the passing weeks they spent hours talking on the phone about life and business. With each late-night conversation, Falyn liked him more and more and anxiously anticipated his nightly call as her favorite part of her day.

Sylvio was like no other man she had ever met. Cool, confident, self-assured and strong. Yet underneath she saw glimpses of his soft underbelly, sweet and sensitive. She had shared her entire sob story with him, and he listened and empathized, but he had yet to share his entire story with her. She had speculated a few things through their conversations, but they were just that, speculations. Sylvio remained a bit of a mystery, even though what he presented to the world was an open book. A book she wanted to read cover to cover.

Just thinking about the handsome man made her hot and bothered: his literal work- of-art body, chiseled and tattooed to bad-boy perfection along with those insanely beautiful blue-grey eyes, so intense and smoldering. How he read her body, knowing exactly what she needed. Falyn had literally come undone by rubbing up on him like a cat in heat, but rather than make her feel awkward about it he made her feel taken care of and cherished in the aftermath. As if she had given him a gift rather than him dishing out an orgasm with no reciprocation. *Had Pierre ever put my pleasure before his own? Never.*

The last of the contractors left for the day, and Falyn closed the door of the guest house, locking it behind her. Just as she did, she heard the loud rumble of a motorcycle and her ears perked up; that familiar sound made her heart race wildly in her chest. She rushed into the great room, seeing Sylvio parked beside the cottage, removing his helmet and running his hand through his disheveled salt and pepper hair. Reaching for the lock on the window, she lifted it and turned the crank to open the window.

"Sylvio!" she shouted through the crack in the window, causing him to pause mid-stride on his way to her cottage door. "Sylvio!" she repeated as he turned towards the calling of his name and smiled, seeing her through the guest house window. She gestured for him to come to the guesthouse, and she made her way to the large front door, unlocking it eagerly and pulling it open. When she did, he was already there, leaning against the cased opening, looking like her wildest, sexiest dream.

"Hi," she said breathlessly at how deliciously handsome he was, in what she had now determined was his usual uniform of tight T-shirts and even tighter jeans topped off with his signature leather jacket.

"Hi, Angel," he said, the sound of his rich voice making her heart skip a beat. "I was just nowhere near your neighborhood and wanted to see you," he said with a wink as he stepped inside and enveloped her in a hug. His signature cologne awakened her senses, and she breathed him in deeply; the smell of him quickly becoming her favorite scent. Releasing their embrace, he asked, "Am I crashing your workday?"

"No, the contractors just left and it's just little old me in this big house," she replied as he stepped further inside, and she closed the door, engaging the lock. His eyes surveyed the front entrance as he walked over to the cased opening of the great room and glanced inside.

"Falyn, this place is incredible. Are those beams original to the house?" he asked, pointing up.

"Yes, apparently they were part of a hip roof barn that once occupied this property and the stone on the fireplace was all sourced from a small quarry just a few miles from here." she said, walking into the great room and spreading out her arms. "It's amazing, isn't it?"

"It is. Wow! Well done," he replied with an approving nod.

"Thanks," she replied, strolling over to him and taking his hand, feathering her fingers with his. "Let me show you my favorite part of this house." Hand in hand she led him back through the front entrance, across the dining room and through the swinging door of the kitchen. Flicking the light switch, the commercial kitchen lit up. The overhead lights reflected off the beautiful, pristine stainless-steel appliances and island countertop. The magnificent gas stove, at the center of it all. "This is my dream kitchen."

Sylvio ran his hand over the stainless steel countertop and walked the perimeter, taking in the fully stocked, fully equipped kitchen. "Looks like a chef's dream to me."

Falyn beamed. "I was just about to make myself dinner here. Would you like to join me?"

"Absolutely," he said, shucking off his leather jacket and hanging it on a hook. Falyn walked over, grabbed her Chef's coat, and slipped it on, buttoning the front and taking a clip from her pocket, twisting up her hair and fastening it at the top of her head.

"I do have one stipulation, though." She said, looking

up at him and setting her hand on his chest. "I need a sous chef."

Sylvio's lips curled into a slow smile. "Done."

Grabbing a basket off the counter, she walked into the cold storage and a moment later walked out with vegetables. Setting the basket down on the counter, she retrieved a bag of flour and a can of San Marzano tomatoes from the cupboard. Then she opened the large refrigerator and set a carton of eggs on the counter, and finally retrieved a large cast-iron Dutch oven. Sylvio's eyes widened as she lifted the lid, and he peered inside.

"Braised short rib," she said. "I made it yesterday when I had a craving and made extra so I could make a short rib ragu."

Sylvio rolled his eyes back, licked his lips, and let out an appreciative groan. "You're after my heart, woman."

Falyn laughed at his reaction, having learned from their conversations that Sylvio was a bit of a foodie and that he too loved to cook when he had the time to.

"Before we make the sauce, we need to make the pasta." She said, setting the flour and eggs beside her. "I could use your muscles for this," she said coyly.

Sylvio mirrored her coyness with a grin and flexed his biceps, making Falyn laugh. She set to work, and he watched as she scooped flour onto the stainless-steel surface, made a well in the middle with her fingers and cracked eggs into the centre. With a fork she slowly broke the egg yolks and incorporated the flour until a loose dough started to form. Gesturing him over, he rounded the island as she gathered up the dough and started to knead.

Sylvio drew impossibly close, towering behind her, his powerful arms bracketing her on either side of the counter. Falyn sucked in a breath, the scent of him swirling in the space between them, the heat between them mounting. He leaned in over her, kneading the dough with the heel of his hand. Instinctively her hands slid on top of his, the solid length of his torso at her back, his pelvis pressing into her behind as the sweltering heat of their attraction radiated between them. He pressed the dough slowly, deliberately, into the counter. Sensually. His forearms strained, the veins and muscles popping as flashbacks of him kneading her breasts with his large hands made desire pool low in her belly. With a quickening pulse, she breathed out. "Just like that."

His hot breath at her ear, he confirmed, "Just like this."

Falyn was on the edge. About to lose control. Scrap the pasta and beg Sylvio to take her right there on her pristine countertop. *How can one man be so impossibly sexy?* She pressed back into him, feeling the unmistakable evidence of his arousal, and it took everything within her not to moan. She needed to regain her self-control.

"That's perfect." She said with a throaty exhale as she shifted away from him. "Now we let it rest in the fridge."

AWARE of how he was teasing and toying with Falyn, Sylvio simply couldn't help himself. All he wanted was to touch her and caress her soft, supple curves. *God, she's sexy.* All five foot four inches of curvy perfection. She didn't hide her attraction towards him either. One look into those gorgeous brown eyes and he saw the effect he had on her. Her eyes were like a mood ring and when she was aroused, they darkened and blazed with a heat so scorching that it took everything in him to not throw her over his shoulder like a caveman, as he took her to the nearest bedroom to act out all his carnal fantasies. Between that and the breathlessness of her voice when he neared her, he was certain she was as affected by him as he was affected by her. Just the sight of her and the sound of her raspy lilt made him rock hard, and he wanted nothing more than to sink himself deep inside her warm, willing body. *But that isn't what she needs right now.* Falyn needed a man that made her feel not only wanted but respected and safe. And if it meant he had to hold back, he would do that, however long it took for her to be ready to take their intimacy further.

Washing his hands, she put him to work chopping carrots, celery, garlic, and onions. He loved to cook, and some of his best memories were in his mother's kitchen. His beautiful Italian mama with her thick Italian accent and warm, bright smile. She would put him and his brother, Antonio, to work chopping, dicing, and stirring. As soon as they were big enough to hold a knife and tall enough to reach the stove, they were recruited to help. Anything to keep them busy and out of trouble.

A melancholy feeling fell over him as he thought about his one and only sibling. He hadn't thought about Antonio in a long time. Sometimes he wondered what he was doing and where he ended up. It had been twenty-five years since they talked, or should he say yelled? Their last words to each other, ones of hurt and anger. Words of ultimate betrayal.

Sylvio glanced up from what he was doing to see Falyn had been watching him. She smiled, gestured to the knife in his hand and the piles of vegetables perfectly diced. "You're good at this."

"I told you I like to cook," he replied with a wink as he went back to work and added. "It's sort of cathartic."

"I agree," she replied, picking up a bowl of shredded short rib and carrying it over to a large cast-iron skillet. "What's your favorite thing to make?"

"Probably my mother's lasagna," he replied. "My mother immigrated from Italy after meeting my father in the military and brought along all her authentic recipes."

"That sounds delicious and romantic. Are they both still around?" Falyn asked, adding the sofrito Sylvio had chopped to a large pan, the sizzle of the fresh vegetables hitting the heated olive oil filling the room.

"No, both have passed. First my father, and shortly thereafter my mother. She never got over my father's passing and, well, I think she just wanted to be with him in the end."

Falyn brought her hand to her heart and let out a swoony sigh. "Now that's true love."

"What about your parents?" he asked, wiping his hands on a towel and folding his arms over his broad chest as he leaned against the countertop.

"Still happily married and as cute as ever," she replied wistfully. "I think after my divorce, I kind of thought that love was this elusive thing. I was completely jaded, and then when I returned home and saw how much my parents still love each other, it made me hopeful."

"Hopeful for what?" he asked, wanting to dive deeper.

"Hopeful that there's still someone out there for me. Someone who gets me and understands what I've been through. Someone who believes in faithfulness and commitment. Honestly, I think commitment is hard to find these days," she added with a resolute shrug.

Sylvio understood her words, having thought similarly in the past. Enduring the breakup of his marriage, the revelation of betrayal and the untimely death of his one and only true love wasn't easy. After he picked up the shattered pieces of his heart, he was certain that love would never find him again. He considered moving on and at times craved having someone who understood him, but having been where he had been and having seen what he had seen, he never was able to fully move on with someone else. He spent the next two decades alone, seeking short-term companionship and fulfilling his desires temporarily. He was never ready, and not until recently had he even considered what a committed relationship might look like. Not until he met Falyn.

"That kind of relationship is hard to find," he agreed. "It's hard to sink your trust in someone when you've had your trust broken."

"Is that why you're still single?" she asked, her gaze meeting his.

"Partially," he replied honestly. "That and until recently I never met someone that interested me that much."

Falyn's eyes flitted from the pot of sauteed vegetables she was stirring to his eyes, and he saw it. She was interested, too. Not just physically, although he had already had a preview at how combustible their chemistry was, but in genuinely getting to know him and see where this thing between them might go. A smile tugged at her lips as she poured in the can of tomatoes, added the garlic and the shredded short rib.

"I like you, Falyn," he said, pushing off the counter and slowly sauntering over to her. Falyn turned, trying to hide her smile as she stirred the contents of the pan, and he rested his hands on her waist. "I like how smart, funny, and ambitious you are. I love that you cook, my God, woman, that smells delicious." he said, looking over her shoulder and inhaling deeply. "And I'm not just saying this, but you may be the most beautiful, sexiest woman I have ever laid eyes on."

Falyn let out a guffaw at that declaration and replied, "You own a bar, Sylvio, I appreciate the compliment, but there's no way I'm the most beautiful or the sexiest."

"All you have to do is look in the mirror, Falyn, and see what I see. You're a stunning woman," he countered.

Falyn shifted out of his hold, and he persisted. "The women in skintight dresses and stilettos that frequent the Pig simply don't do it for me," he replied, sliding his hands over the curve of her hips. "I happen to like a real woman with soft, natural curves." He said, turning her around to face him as he continued. "And nothing is sexier than a woman with pretty little freckles on her nose." Sylvio leaned down, her eyes fluttering closed as he planted an affectionate kiss on the bridge of her nose. Falyn shivered, a subtle vibration radiating through her body and surging into his. Sylvio loved the way she responded at the slightest touch, and when her eyes opened, rising slowly to meet him, only one question needed to be asked. "Do you like me, Falyn?"

FALYN'S SKIN HEATED. Sylvio intoxicated her and made her feel lightheaded, as if floating on big fluffy clouds. He was simply complimenting her, and she was now a melted puddle on her kitchen floor. Sylvio saw her, appreciated her just as she was, and by the look in his eyes, he desired her as much as she desired him. All things she now in retrospect never really felt in her marriage. Her relationship with Pierre seemed to be more of a business transaction, with sex thrown in to appease her. *Did he ever truly desire me?* Or did he see her culinary talent and know exactly what to say and what to do to keep her where he wanted her. In his kitchen, making him money, and when she was home in his bed, satisfying the itch until he could be with his flavor of the month. After they split, tales of his trysts circled back to her from friends, colleagues and acquaintances. Hearing about them made her feel naïve and stupid, blinded by an exotically handsome face, a dream job and the promise of a glamorous life.

She broke out of her thoughts and gazed deep into the pools of Sylvio's steely eyes. Eyes she could so easily drown in if she wasn't careful. A man who had the potential to break her heart if she opened it to him, and yet, as she repeated his question to herself and searched his gaze, a deep sense of calm fell over her. Because of what she knew so far about Sylvio, that he was a good and honest man, she was certain beyond a shadow of a doubt that he would never do anything to intentionally hurt her.

"I like you too, Sylvio. Very much," she replied, sliding her hands around his waist and giving him a wary look. "I'm just scared of letting someone in. I know you understand that."

"I do," he replied, pinning her with his compassionate gaze. "I need you to know, Falyn, I will always respect you. Whether we explore where things could go or simply stay friends. If you choose to trust me, I will protect your heart."

Falyn searched his eyes, only to find truth and honesty in their depths. "I want to try with you, Sylvio."

"Then let's date and see where this takes us, no timelines, no expectations, just two people that mutually like each other and are wildly attracted to each other," he said, brushing a curl from her cheek and caressing it softly with his fingers. "Does this mean I can kiss you whenever I want?"

Falyn threw her head back in laughter and replied, "Yes, but not until we eat."

Volleying back with a laugh of his own, Sylvio conceded as he released his hold on her, and she retrieved the pasta dough from the refrigerator. By the time they were done prepping and cooking dinner, they were laughing and covered in flour with two heaping bowls of rich and meaty pasta as they sat on the counter, feet dangling off the edge.

"This might be the best thing I've ever put in my mouth." Sylvio mumbled with a mouthful and an appreciative nod. Falyn cocked an eyebrow at him, and he chuckled deeply. "Well, maybe the second-best thing."

Falyn grinned, looking down at the bowl of pasta in her hand with a question she was itching to ask on the tip of her tongue. "Speaking of that. Do you make it a habit to invite yourself over to a woman's house only to have her dry hump you?"

Sylvio nearly choked on a bite, chewed, then let out a huge, bountiful laugh that echoed through her kitchen as he answered. "The answer would be no, and may I ask what the context of this question is? Because I'm pretty sure if I slid my fingers into your panties while you straddled my lap, there would have been nothing dry about it." Her core clenched at his dirty words. *Damn my traitorous body.* He went on snaring her with his intense gaze. "I'm pretty sure you're turned on right now too, aren't you, Falyn?"

With his question, Sylvio set down his bowl of pasta and hopped off the counter, turning to face her. Falyn felt her entire body flush with heat as he pinned her with his sexy stare. Coming closer, he ran his hands over her knees to her thighs and back down again before inching them apart and nestling himself at her apex. Plucking the bowl from her hand, he set it next to his and slowly ran his large hands over her shoulders and down over her back to her behind, pulling her closer in one sharp move. Her breath caught, and she sucked it in between her teeth, his hard muscled chest in her face as she looked up to meet his wanton gaze. "Do I turn you on?" he asked again.

"Yes," she rasped as his large palm came up and cupped her cheek.

"Because you turn me on so fucking much, it's hard to keep from taking you right here on this countertop." Sylvio growled. An inadvertent moan escaped her lips as he drew closer, his mouth hovering over hers. "To answer your question, no, I don't make it a habit. I'm a one-woman man, and you, Falyn, are the one I want." With those words, he lowered his tantalizing lips to hers in a sensual, mind-melding kiss.

Heat surged through Sylvio's body as his tongue slipped past the seam of Falyn's mouth and slid against hers. He grabbed her behind and pressed her core into his painfully hard groin, wanting, needing to get closer. He couldn't get enough of her: her eyes, her halo of soft blonde curls, that gorgeous smile and her decadent, pillowy lips. Then there was her body, that sang out to him. A sweet song only his body could hear. Her the treble to his bass. Together, a perfect melody.

God, I want her. All of her. But he wasn't going to go that far, even though his body screamed for release. Being with Falyn was going to mean more. More to her and certainly more to him. Because as he kissed and caressed this remarkable woman, in his heart he was certain he was starting to fall.

CHAPTER 6

Falyn entered her parents' farmhouse; the smell of beef roast, Yorkshire pudding, potatoes and rich dark gravy wafted from the kitchen. Walking into the kitchen, her father was standing behind her mother, his hands on her shoulders as she stirred the pot of gravy on the stove. The roast sat on a cutting board, ready to be carved. Falyn leaned against the doorjamb and watched them for a moment. Her father leaned down, planted a kiss on her mother's cheek, and her mother swatted him away as she let out a giggle. *They are far too cute.*

Immediately her mind went to how Sylvio stood behind her, hands on her hips while she stirred the sauce for their pasta, and she smiled. Last night they had cooked together, enjoyed the pasta, engaged in rousing conversation, and made out like a couple of horny teenagers on her kitchen counter. Everything about their evening together was perfect. Touching her lips at the memory, she hadn't noticed her parents had turned to see her.

"Hi there, Sweetheart. I didn't hear you come in." Her mother said, setting the gravy on the table.

"You look deep in thought, Cookie," her father said, picking up the carving knife and fork and starting to carve the roast into perfect thin slices.

"Yeah, sorry, just a lot on my mind. Prairie Charm opens next weekend, and I constantly have to-do lists running through my head." She replied. *Actually, Mom and Dad. I was thinking about the hot as hell, two decades my senior man that I'm dating who had his tongue down my throat last night.* Falyn shook the naughty response from her head. As far as she was concerned, they were on a need-to-know basis with regard to her new relationship with Sylvio.

"Your brother is bringing a woman he's seeing named Kaitlyn for dinner, and we all need to be on our best behavior," her mother said, glancing over at her father and giving him a chiding look. "He seems to like her, and we don't want to scare her off."

"Brooks is seeing someone?" Falyn asked, washing her hands at the kitchen sink and grabbing dinner plates from the cupboard. "I must be out of the loop."

"Yes, he's been dating this woman for a little while now, sometime after his birthday, I think. Honestly, when he told me he was seeing someone, I assumed it was Georgie," her mother answered with a sigh.

"Poor boy, got tired of waiting," her father piped in. "Honestly, I just wish those two would figure it out."

Falyn had to agree, her brother and his best friend Georgie would be perfect together, and although her brother had made it clear that he wanted more than friendship, Georgie was a harder sell.

"Hey!" the booming voice of her brother echoed through the house. "We're here." Her big and tall brother entered the kitchen, a pretty, petite woman with dark hair and dark eyes following behind him. Brooks put his arm around the woman, whose long, straight hair was pulled back in a tight ponytail. "This is Kaitlyn."

Brooks made introductions, and although Falyn's immediate impression of Kaitlyn was that she was very sweet and pleasant, she could see her brother wasn't happy. And as they ate dinner, her loud, boisterous family filled the small kitchen space with laughter, animated conversation and the usual disagreements or debates. All it took was one look at Kaitlyn to see that she wasn't comfortable with their kind of crazy family. Falyn understood, having gone through the introductions with Pierre when they got serious and his refusal to come home with her after they were married, stating he wasn't used to their family dynamic. They were a lot, but she wouldn't have it any other way.

Sylvio would fit in here. The thought immediately struck her. *But would he? What would her parents think about her dating someone so much older than her? Would they be concerned or pull her aside, warning her not to get caught up with someone again that has the potential to hurt her?* Sylvio wasn't like that though. He was a protector and an honorable man. He had promised her as much last night. Yet, the thought of introducing them to Sylvio made her pulse spike and anxiety fill her body.

"Falyn," Brooks said, breaking her from her waring

thoughts. "I saw a motorcycle parked beside your cottage last night when I was driving by. The lights of the guest-house were on, and it was late. Was one of the contractors working there late last night?"

Busted. I'm not ready for this. A little white lie never hurt anyone. "Ah, kind of. I was giving someone a tour of the guest house." *That was partially true, although we didn't seem to make it past the kitchen counter.* A slow blush started to creep up her neck and settle in her cheeks. She flashed her brother a glaring look, knowing the only way to get out of this conversation was distraction.

"I have my first event at Prairie Charm coming up. Kolt and Jane's rehearsal dinner. They want me to come up with a menu, and they expect around 30 guests for dinner. What do you think? Prime Rib or Coq au vin?"

This started a heated debate about the best dishes Falyn could cook, and she caught Brooks' gaze in her peripheral vision. He was smirking, the look on his face saying, "Well played". Falyn had some explaining to do, but for now the attention on her and Sylvio had been diverted.

* * *

OPENING weekend for Prairie Charm Bed and Breakfast had finally arrived, and Falyn was both excited and nervous. Friday guests started arriving, the booked rooms filling as they settled in and started roaming the guest house and grounds. Part of the renovation of the property was building herself a garage and fencing off one corner of the lawn so that she could have a private space that was just hers. The rest of the lawn was set up with nice seating areas, a fire pit, and lawn games like cornhole and bocce ball.

The comments from her guests were lovely and kind as they took in the large great room and marveled at the tall, beamed ceilings and beautiful stone fireplace. Falyn had curated brochures from local businesses encouraging them to explore Primrose, and so far, everything was going swimmingly. Later that evening, back in her kitchen, she started prep work for the first breakfast that would start being served at 8 a.m. Thick Belgian waffles, vanilla custard with berry compote, light and fluffy herb scrambled eggs, baked hash browns with onions and peppers, along with fat, juicy sausages and crispy bacon, were on the menu. For those wanting a lighter breakfast, baked oatmeal, cups of fresh fruit and, of course, a selection of pastries from Everything You Knead.

The swinging door of her kitchen opened, and in walked Sylvio, his helmet under his arm. "Hey there, Angel," he said, looking so handsome and suave her heart leaped. *Was it ever going to get old looking at this man?*

"What are you doing here?" She asked, setting her knife down and rounding the island to greet him. "Fridays are a busy night at the Pig."

"They are, but my assistant manager and head bartender have it covered. I told them I had somewhere I needed to be for the weekend," he said, wrapping her up in a hug. "I figured you could use my help."

Falyn sighed, his warmth and masculine cologne now her greatest source of comfort. "You didn't need to do that."

"I know. But I wanted to," he replied, leaning down and planting a chaste kiss on her lips. "I'm here as long as you need me, so put me to work."

Falyn laughed. "I'm almost done for tonight, but will need to be up early to get breakfast going at 8 a.m."

"So, no late night make-out session?" he asked with a wink, his lips curved into a knowing smile.

"I never said that," she volleyed, making his smile grow wider.

They finished up the rest of the prep and when the kitchen was clean, they did a sweep of the great room, grounds and slowly walked to her cottage, hand in hand. Sylvio retrieved a small leather bag strapped to the back of his bike, and Falyn opened the door, Sylvio following behind.

Setting his bag down, he slipped out of his leather jacket and hung it up at the door, grabbing his bag and setting it down on a chair. "I'm happy to sleep here," he said, gesturing to the couch. "I know you only have one bedroom."

"What if I told you I wanted you in my bed?" Falyn asked, slowly approaching him and smoothing her hand around his waist and under the hem of his t-shirt.

"I'd say, your wish is my command," he replied, his brows drawing together as he added. "I don't want you to feel pressure to do anything though. I'll wait as long as you need."

Falyn gazed up at him through her long lashes as she lifted his T-shirt up, exposing his magnificent body and beautiful ink. "I could really use a shower. Are you going to join me?"

* * *

SYLVIO'S PULSE QUICKENED, and his jeans tightened. His growing member pressed painfully against his zipper. This wasn't why he came here tonight, but he wasn't about to deny this incredible woman what she wanted. Everything about Falyn turned him on, and although he was willing to wait as long as it took for her to be comfortable with them taking their chemistry to the next level, he was ready and more than willing if that time was now.

Falyn shed his shirt, tossing it to the couch, and started unbuttoning her blouse as she backed towards the bathroom. Slipping off her blouse, she discarded it and started unbuttoning her jeans. He followed like a predator zoning in on his prey as he undid the button of his jeans and expertly shucked them, leaving him in his boxer briefs. Falyn bit her bottom lip as she looked her fill, and a wicked smile curled her lips as she slipped her jeans over her hips, exposing a minuscule pair of bikini underwear. Reaching behind her for the clasp of her bra, she let it slide down her arms and off, causing a low growl to reverberate from Sylvio's throat.

"You have the most beautiful breasts," he complimented, his eyes feasting on them.

She smiled coyly, now at the door of the bathroom as she hooked her fingers into the sides of her underwear and slowly drew them down her legs and off. Sylvio took her in, the expanse of her creamy bare flesh, all curvy, sexy, natural perfection. Not wanting to leave her vulnerable and exposed, he slid his briefs slowly down his hips and off, freeing his manhood, standing tall and proud. Her eyes drifted over him, lingering at the evidence of his desire for her, long, thick and weeping for the warmth of her body. Falyn's eyes flared with appreciation as her tongue flicked out, moistening her bottom lip, and her eyes slowly drifted up to meet his, reflecting pure, untamed passion in their depths.

Drawing closer, she cocked a brow at him and took his hand as she led him into the shower. Falyn started the shower, adjusting the spray and turned, meeting his wanton gaze. Sylvio gripped her hips, kneading the flesh with his fingers as he turned her towards the wall and caged her against it. His long, taut body radiated heat and pressed into her, causing a moan to escape her lips. The intensity of her gaze scorched him as he bent down and took a taut nipple into his mouth, sucking it hard. Falyn arched her back and moaned loudly, fisting his hair as he trailed hot kisses to the other breast and gave it equal attention. Kissing his way down her stomach, he fell to his knees, his mouth watering as he neared her core. Lifting one leg over his shoulder and the other over the opposite shoulder, leaving her to brace herself against the shower wall, he looked up, meeting her gaze with hungry eyes. "I got you."

"Sylvio," she whimpered. "You don't have to."

"And miss the appetizer? Not a chance. I need to taste you, Falyn. See if you're as sweet as I think you are," he said, before he buried his face between her thighs. Her sex was rosy, ripe, and open to him. Sweeping his tongue through her satin folds, she gasped, the sound echoing off the tiles of the shower. *Just as I suspected, sweet like honey.*

Trailing his eyes up her perfect body, he curled his lips into a wicked grin and met her needy gaze. "Delicious."

* * *

FALYN'S HEAD spun as Sylvio dived in, feasting on her with abandon. She had done this act many times in her life, but never had a man so thoroughly licked, teased and toyed with her like this. It was so erotic, how he held her up, strong and powerful, and consumed her like a dying man searching for his final meal. How the scruff on his chin rasped deliciously against the sensitive skin of her thighs and core. How the vortex of her release started to build; a fast-moving storm ready to unleash. Sylvio didn't relent, finding her pleasure center, first teasing it with his tongue, then expertly taking it between his lips and drawing it in. She gasped as she arched her back off the wall of the shower, her pelvis pressing into his face, her legs clamping around his head.

"I'm coming." She cried, unable to stop the sweet crescendo of her orgasm. Stars formed behind her eyes, and for a moment she lost all sense of time and place. He didn't stop, just held her up, lapping feverishly until she came down from the peak. Carefully setting her back down on her feet, he rose and caught her as her knees wobbled and she melted into him, his arms coming around her protectively. Falyn met his gaze, a rush of unexpected emotion rising in her chest. Seeing this, Sylvio cupped her face, caressing the soft skin of her cheeks She sighed, melting into his tender touch and willing the tears away by closing her eyes.

"I haven't been with anyone since my ex-husband." Falyn explained, her voice shaky, her eyes unable to meet his gaze. "It's hard not to get in your head a little when you've been cheated on."

"I know the feeling," he replied, brushing the curls from her eyes. "But you did nothing wrong. You know that, right? You simply fell for the wrong man. A man who didn't appreciate or deserve you."

"And you're the right man?" she asked.

"I'd like to be."

Falyn opened her eyes and gazed up into his beautiful stare, seeing raw honesty reflected there. The more time she spent with Sylvio, the more she wanted him to be that too. Sylvio was very quickly repairing the hole in her heart, left from her messy divorce. A deep, cavernous hole she never thought anyone could ever fill until he came along, so unexpectedly. An incredible man, who was sweet and sensitive and who saw and understood her. A man she already, after such a short time, trusted with her heart. A man she was starting to fall for.

Reaching for the shampoo, he gestured for her to spin around,, and she gave him a confused look. "Let me take care of you tonight," he said, squirting shampoo into his palms. She conceded, turning as his firm fingers massaged the shampoo into her scalp. Giving into his request, she moaned as he washed her hair, then grabbed the loofah and washed her body, caressing tenderly as he went. She melted at his touch, and when he was done, he lifted her out of the shower and towel-dried her, slowly and reverently. She let him, giving in to him fully, and something about her complete surrender felt reverent. A poignant moment of trust between them. Fully dried, he scooped her into his arms and carried her into the bedroom, pulling back the covers and laying her on the cool sheets. She shivered as he slipped in next to her and pulled her into him, encasing her in the warmth of his strong, naked body. She fit against his body so seamlessly, and before long, her eyes grew heavy, sleep overtaking them both as they remained wrapped in each other's embrace.

CHAPTER 7

Sylvio jerked awake, immediately glancing around the room, seeing Falyn had rolled over and was sleeping on her side facing away from him. He glanced over her shoulder to ensure he hadn't woken her and slid his legs out of the bed, resting them on the wooden floor. Leaning forward, he ran his hands through his hair, trying to concentrate on breathing and wiping the dream from his consciousness. He hated this dream. A dream that had haunted him for decades. Charity, her lifeless body in his truck. *Why hadn't I locked the garage? Why hadn't I heard the engine running?* The nightmare plagued him on and off for years after her death, and he couldn't understand why it was coming back now. It had been decades since Charity took her life. Decades before, she had entered his garage, found his keys still in the ignition and climbed into his truck, starting the engine. Decades after she'd closed her eyes and let the carbon monoxide fill her lungs. Finding her the next morning, limp and cold. No note, no explanation.

Falyn turned, curling her dainty hands under her cheek as she hugged her pillow, and he smiled. She looked angelic even in the darkness of the room. *Man, I'm falling fast for her.* Over the past six weeks he seemed to measure things in two timelines: before Falyn and after Falyn. Before Falyn, he was a lonely bar owner who honestly wasn't looking for commitment. Was just content to let the chips fall where they may, and if he ended up alone for the rest of his life, so be it. After Falyn, he woke up each day, wondering what she was doing and when he would see her next. He thought about her constantly. Meeting her had made him seriously think about the rest of his life and how he wanted nothing more than to share it with someone. How he was done being a lone wolf. Falyn represented beauty and light, and he needed that in his life. Perhaps for the rest of his life.

"Is everything okay?" a small, raspy voice asked in the darkness, and he turned as Falyn lifted her head from her pillow and sat up, clutching the comforter to her bare chest. "Can't sleep?"

"No, it's okay, Angel, I just had a dream that woke me. Go back to bed, I'll be right back."

Falyn lay her head back down on the pillow, and he rose, walking to the bedroom door, leaving it open a crack as he made his way into the kitchen. Opening cupboards, he found tumblers and poured himself a glass of cold water, letting it soothe him as he stared out the kitchen window over the darkened lawn of Prairie Charm. Warm, slender hands curled around his waist, and Falyn kissed his back. He closed his eyes, emotion rising in his chest at the tenderness of her touch. He would consider himself a sensitive man, but he didn't like his vulnerability to show, and right now, he felt beyond vulnerable. Falyn seemed to sense it and he clutched her hands to his body as she rested her cheek on his back. They stood there for a while, naked, emotionally exposed and bathed in the moonlight from the kitchen window until Falyn broke the silence.

"Let's go back to bed," she said softly as she took his hand and led him back to her bed. No more words needed to be said.

THE NEXT MORNING, they rose early to get started on the first breakfast and brunch at Prairie Charm Bed and Breakfast. Falyn was excited to spoil her guests with her cooking, and from the smiles and nods from her guests as they ate, and the compliments that followed, a deep sense of pride enveloped her at what she had created here. Having gone from the executive chef at a popular Vancouver restaurant to an owner and chef at a small-town bed and breakfast was undeniably a change, but seeing the happy faces confirmed that she had made the right choice in coming back home.

She glanced over at Sylvio, going from table to table filling up coffee cups, talking and laughing with her guests. He was a natural, and although she was aware that he was good with a crowd, seeing him adapt to such a contrasting environment from his bar was unexpected. Selfishly, she wished she could have him here every weekend.

With everything running smoothly in the dining room, Falyn escaped to the kitchen, pouring herself a cup of coffee and leaning against her kitchen island. Last night had been unexpected in more ways than one. As soon as Sylvio showed up and she realized he was going to be spending the weekend, the desire to explore their intimacy wasn't even in question. But having him take care of her like that, and not asking for anything in return, was surprising. She had never had a man give without the expectation of taking. There was always a very clear tit for tat.

Falyn tugged at the collar of her chef's coat and bit her bottom lip. Just the thought of his scruff scraping her thighs, his long, luscious tongue exploring the sensitive crevice between her legs and how he expertly teased where she pulsed. No one had ever made her come that hard before with oral sex. Falyn's face flushed with the memory, and a wicked thought crossed her mind. They had another night together, and tonight was going to be all about him.

THEY RETIRED to her cottage at the end of the day, both exhausted and happy with how the day went. Deciding to unwind on the couch with a movie, Falyn excused herself to change into pajamas. Entering her bedroom, she beelined for her dresser, knowing exactly what she was going to put on. Sliding the drawer open, she lifted the practical pajamas and buried underneath was a black lace lingerie set she bought for herself after her divorce was finalized. She was walking towards her car outside her lawyer's office, and she passed a boutique, seeing this sexy two-piece set in the window. She had never cared for lingerie, but something made her stop and admire the exquisite detail and lace. After being betrayed and the subsequent grueling months of divorce negotiations, she needed to feel pretty and sexy again, so she marched right into that boutique, tried it on and bought it without hesitation. She had forgotten all about it until today and after last night's orgasmic mind-blowing shower, she wanted to lay the groundwork for her own seduction.

Slipping out of her clothes, she put on the set and surveyed herself in the mirror. The two-piece bralette and lace-trimmed short set accentuated her curves and petite hourglass figure to perfection. Reaching for her jasmine perfume, she spritzed it in the air, walked through the mist, and set it back down on her dresser. Head held high, she fluffed up her curls, her pulse quickening as she entered the living room. Sylvio's eyes were on the TV as he flipped through channels and took a sip from a can of Coke he had retrieved from the fridge. As she boldly rounded the side of the couch, his eyes caught on her as he slowly lowered the can from his mouth and swallowed, his Adam's apple bobbing as he did. Nonchalantly, she sauntered over to him, making sure to sway her hips a little more than usual, and stood in front of him, bringing her hands to her hips and cocking one out to the side. He leaned back against the couch, slouching ever so slightly, parting his legs further apart as his eyes drifted over her slowly, deliberately, taking in her scantily clad body.

"Holy shit," he said, his voice coming out low and gravelly. "Are you a dream?"

She fell to her knees in front of him, widening his legs and running her hands over his thick, muscular thighs. "A dirty dream, yes," she replied, meeting his gaze and running her palm over the growing bulge in his jeans. Reaching for his belt, he watched her unfasten it, his eyes growing dark with desire, as she pulled it out of the loops with one swoop. He growled at her show of dominance as she took his belt and looped the leather around the back of his neck, pulling him in closer so she could capture his lips. She kissed him, deep and passionate, coaxing his tongue to tangle with hers as he reached to pull her up onto his lap. Peeling her lips away, she put her finger up, shaking it from side to side, scolding him. "Not yet. You gave to me so generously last night. It's my turn to return the favor."

* * *

Am I dreaming? Sylvio met Falyn's lustful gaze as he watched her lower his zipper seductively and coax his jeans over his behind and down his thick thighs. Lifting his hips, she hooked her fingers into the waistband of his briefs and slowly slid them down, freeing his hard steel length. Her eyes dilated, almost black, as she curled her hand around his shaft, bowed her head and swirled her tongue around his crown, capturing the evidence of his arousal at the tip. He tried to breathe as she gripped him, pumping once, twice, then lowering her head again to take him into her warm, wet mouth. He was large by all standards; he was aware of that, but Falyn hollowed out her cheeks and took him to the hilt, hitting the back of her throat.

"Fuck." he growled, the deep sound coming from his throat wild and feral, as she set a steady rhythm, sliding him in and out of her expert mouth, teasing the head and diving back in as she swirled her tongue around his length. It took all his self-control to not take over and drive his hips into her warm and willing mouth, but he held back, allowing her to take full control. Quickly that slow burn of his orgasm coiled tight, like a rubber band about to let go, his balls tightening as she caressed them while sucking him deep. She moaned as she took him to the hilt again, and that was all it took for the band to break. Like a slingshot, it ricocheted through his body, and there was no time to pull away. She was going to take all of him and drink him down. There was no slowing down. As his orgasm peaked, she swallowed, taking all he had to give, and when he was done, she licked him like a lollipop, capturing every last drop as she met his gaze through her long dark lashes, a look of naughty accomplishment on her face.

Rising to her feet, she straddled his lap and reached for the hem of his T-shirt, lifting it over his head. She smiled at him as he tried to regain his composure, and she traced down the lines of his tattoos with her fingertips. "You are the most extraordinary woman I have ever met. That was hands down the best blowjob of my life."

Falyn laughed lightly, running her hands over his pecs as she rocked over his lap. "Have you had a lot of blowjobs?" she asked curiously.

"More than my share," he replied. "I haven't been celibate if that's what you're asking."

She nodded, sliding her thumbs over his nipples and making them peak. "When was your last sexual encounter?"

"About a year ago," he replied. "I dated a woman for around two months. She was older than me, actually, and was looking for commitment. I wasn't."

"So, you broke it off?" Falyn asked.

"She did. She was a nice woman, sweet, beautiful, but I couldn't see us working past casual dating," he answered truthfully.

"When was your last relationship?" she asked.

"My ex-wife."

"That's a long time," Falyn replied.

"Yes, but truthfully no one ever came into my life that I wanted to get serious with," he responded, cupping her behind and pulling her closer. "Until I met you."

"You want that with me?" she asked, a slow smile curling her lips. "A relationship."

"More than anything," Sylvio replied. "I've never met anyone like you, Falyn. I can't get enough of you."

She cupped his face and kissed him passionately, pressing him against the back of the couch, her pert breasts sliding against the hard ridges of his chest. Pulling her lips away, she stared into his eyes and spoke. "I can't get enough of you too, and I want more of you." She took his hand and brought it down to her sex. "Feel what you do to me, Sylvio," she insisted, guiding his long, large fingers past her bottoms to her wet, swollen flesh. "You have me dripping and begging to be filled."

* * *

What has come over me? Falyn had always considered herself a sex-positive woman, but the brazen words that were coming out of her mouth were surprising even to her. She needed him. Wanted him. Craved to have his hard steel length stretch her to her limits. To drive her to the edge of ecstasy and make her fall.

Sylvio's body hardened, rubbing against the panel of her bottoms as he removed his fingers and drew them to his mouth. Bringing her sweetness to his lips. The move was so erotic; it made Falyn's heart beat outside her chest. There was no stopping this; she was going to have him. Have him now. Taking charge, she pulled aside the panel of her lingerie bottoms and gripped his rock-hard shaft that pulsed in her hand. Rising, she rubbed the crown through her wetness, teasing the bundle of nerves and poised him at her entrance. With his lust-drunk eyes locked on hers, she sank down, taking all of him deep inside her body. A pleasurable pain radiated through her core as she stretched, her muscles accommodating the length and girth of his swollen member. She sucked in a breath slowly, exhaling as she glanced down, all of him entirely buried in her warm, wanton body. Looking up, his eyes were closed, his breath coming out stuttered.

"Are you okay?" she asked, brows drawing together in question.

"It just feels so fucking good. So tight and warm. Oh fuck, Falyn, you feel too damn amazing." He managed on a breath, opening his eyes, dark with desire. "How do you want it, Angel? Slow and gentle or hard and dirty?"

She steadied her hands on his broad shoulders and rose until he was almost out and slid back down, causing them both to moan loudly with pleasure. "Hard and dirty," she answered with a shuddering gasp. "Don't be gentle."

"Good answer," he replied wickedly as he thrust from underneath, lifting his ass off the couch, his powerful legs giving him leverage.

"Oh, God!" she cried as he lifted her, guiding her movements and unrelentingly claimed her body again and again. Hitting places in her that had never been touched. Everything about their coupling was raw and carnal as he guided her body, taking her fast and hard, bringing her higher with each powerful thrust of his hips. All she could do was grip his shoulders and savor the mounting pleasure in her building fast and furious. The unbridled sounds escaping her lips indicated she was close to letting go.

"Please tell me you're close, Angel, I can't hold out much longer," he gritted between his teeth on yet another punishing thrust.

"Do that again," she pleaded, throwing her head back and pushing her breasts forward. Roughly pulling down a cup of the bralette, Sylvio wrapped his lips around a pebbled peak, sucking her deep. She cried out, arching her back as her orgasm consumed her. The tight heat of her internal muscles spasming in luxurious waves around his hard steel.

"Fuck!" he cursed as she felt him swell impossibly larger inside her and with one more delicious slide erupt deep inside her body.

She collapsed on him, her hips rocking out the last of

her release, their bodies slick with sweat, evidence of their mutual release coating their thighs. They both trembled with aftershocks as he wrapped his strong arms around her and held her close.

Suddenly, he shifted underneath her, sliding out of her body, and she raised her head to be met with eyes full of concern.

"We didn't use protection," he said, his voice rough. "Fuck, Falyn, please tell me you are on birth control."

Falyn smiled down at him, appreciating his concern and smoothing her thumbs over the creases between his brows. "I have an IUD and considering the demise of my marriage, I was recently tested."

"I get tested every year," he replied, letting out an exhale of relief. "Are you sure you're okay going bare, because I don't know about you, but I want to do that again."

Falyn nodded and giggled, burying her head in his neck and nibbling on his ear as she whispered. "Sleep is overrated."

CHAPTER 8

The next morning, Falyn and Sylvio were up extra early not only for the bed and breakfast guests but also for the invitation-only brunch thereafter. With the extra prep, Falyn was grateful for an extra pair of hands. Hands that knew exactly where and how she liked to be touched. Her core clenched as she thought about the night before, how after the fast, dirty sex on the couch, he carried her to the bed, stripped off the lingerie and kissed every inch of her skin. Then he sank back into her heat, the feel of his hard, strong body hovering over her as he brought her to two more back-to-back orgasms, slowly drawing out her pleasure and his own.

Falyn glanced over at Sylvio, contentedly chopping and dicing as she instructed. His eyes rose to meet hers, and he smiled, the lines next to his eyes deepening, making her heart do a little flip-flop. *I like this man. I like him a lot. What will my family say? Will they like him too?* Falyn didn't know. She had never paid much mind to other people's opinions, taking the stance that their opinions were none of her business, but this was different. She was opening herself and Sylvio to scrutiny, and that bothered her.

"What's wrong?" Sylvio asked, noticing her change in demeanor, his brows furrowing with his question.

"My family and friends are going to be here for the brunch," she said quietly as she gulped down, trying to figure out the best way to approach this with Sylvio.

"Awesome. I assume Brooks and your parents will be here," he replied, going back to his prep work.

"Yeah, and I haven't told them about you yet," she confessed, suddenly feeling the need to scramble out an explanation. "It's not that I'm hiding the fact that we're dating, but my parents are kind of protective since my marriage broke up and well, and I'm honestly not sure how they will respond. They certainly won't be expecting me to be in a relationship."

"Does Brooks know?" he asked curiously.

"I think he suspects, yes."

"Then don't worry about it. Until you're ready, let's just tell people we're friends," he suggested, meeting her wary gaze.

"Are you sure? I don't want you to think this thing between us isn't important to me," she replied, her brows knit together. "You really are important to me, Sylvio."

Sylvio wiped his hands on a towel and rounded the island, coming towards her. She set down her knife and turned to face him as he rested his hands on her hips and leaned in, planting a soft, sweet kiss on her lips. Pulling away, he gazed down at her, his blue-grey eyes sparkling. "I respect whatever you decide, Falyn. If you want to share about us, great; if you're not ready, then don't. It doesn't change the way I feel about you."

"How do you feel about me?" she asked, searching his eyes.

"Like my heart seeks yours."

Falyn's eyes softened with his words, and those three sacred words sat on the tip of her tongue. *It's too soon. Don't do it.* "I… I adore you, Sylvio."

A slow smile painted across his face, and he leaned in and planted another chaste kiss to her lips before giving her a reassuring nod and returning to his prep work on the other side of the island.

* * *

LOOKING AROUND THE DINING ROOM, Sylvio grinned, immense pride washing over him at what Falyn had accomplished. The bed and breakfast was beautiful, and the food even better. *My girlfriend is talented. My girlfriend.* He hadn't used that label since Charity, and even then, she had become his wife so fast that the label didn't last long. His eyes met Falyn's from across the room and a smile tugged at her lips, his heart melting. For the first time in decades, he wanted nothing more than to be a boyfriend.

"So, you and my sister are friends?" Brooks asked, taking a seat next to him and setting down his plate. "She said you've been helping her with the business."

"Yeah, I mean she's bounced things off me. I've acquired some business wisdom over the years, so I might as well share it," Sylvio answered, looking Brooks in the eye.

Brooks offered him an appreciative grin. "Well, thank you. My sister has been through a lot, and she deserves something and someone good in her life. I'm glad she has you," Brooks added, giving him a sly wink as he leaned in, his eyes pinned to Sylvio's. "But if you hurt her, I'll kick your ass."

Sylvio chuckled and leaned towards him to respond. "I would expect nothing less."

* * *

FOR THE FIRST time in Falyn's life, she had built something that was truly hers. Prairie Charm was receiving rave reviews and more and more calls for reservations kept coming in. According to many of her fellow business owners in town, they too had experienced a noticeable increase in traffic, so the benefits of helping her small town had its own satisfaction.

Then there was her relationship with Sylvio. Although their time together was limited, when they were together, their endless conversation and laughter left her feeling intellectually stimulated and giddy as a schoolgirl. The significant age difference between them had become a moot point. Sylvio had a way of making her feel youthful, playful, and so much more like the woman she was before she went to Vancouver and got caught up in Pierre's world. Between the carefree feeling he brought to her life and the intense, raw sexual chemistry between them, she finally felt like the young, virile woman she should be.

Although she and Sylvio were all in on their relationship and she trusted him implicitly, there were still a few mysteries about him that perplexed her. The first of which was his relationship with his ex-wife. From his indication, she was no longer a part of his life, which she surmised was due to the betrayal in their marriage. Yet what she couldn't figure out was the look in his eye when he talked about her. He'd shared details about their marriage, how she had cheated, ultimately ending their five years together and how devastated he was in the aftermath. Yet when she met his gaze, she saw a deep, dark sadness there. Not the kind of disappointed sadness one feels when a marriage ends, but a sorrowful sadness when suffering a great and tragic loss. Like the death of someone you love. Recognizing the look in his eye, she chose not to question further, but deep down in her heart she was certain there was more to the story that he wasn't ready to share. *But would he ever be ready to share? Does he trust me as much as I trust him? Would he open the book of his life and share that chapter with me, no matter how dark and twisted it was?* Something inside her told her that if he did, their relationship would flourish, but if he didn't, she wasn't sure how far it could go. That scared her a little if she was being honest with herself. The post-traumatic effects of having a lying, cheating ex-husband she supposed. Maybe that's why she chose to keep her relationship with Sylvio on a need-to-know basis for so long.

After her marriage broke up, with Pierre's infidelity at the center, her loved ones were aware that there were other issues that tore them apart as well. Issues like lifestyle and cultural differences, him having been raised by an affluent European family and her from humble beginnings on a prairie poultry farm. The largest of their issues was when or if to start a family. The family issue became clear shortly after they were married, with Pierre stalling the conversation for the first few years then making it very clear that he didn't see children in his future. That whole declaration gutted her. At that point, Falyn's whole world had revolved around him and the restaurant so Falyn had only two choices; end their marriage and give up not only the man but her dream job, or sacrifice her desire to be a mother if she wanted to stay with him and keep said job. She chose the latter and, in the end, of course she regretted her choice wholeheartedly. Falyn couldn't bear the thought of that happening again. Entering a committed relationship with questions only to find out answers that she couldn't live with.

Then there was the elephant in the room. The age gap. Would her family see her sacrificing all over again because of Sylvio's age? Stereotypically, men of Sylvio's age didn't have the desire to start families, and because of this she was scared to ask. Falyn didn't know where he stood on the topic and what he saw for his future. So, considering the short time they'd been dating, she didn't want anything to pop her happy little bubble, choosing to push that topic aside until the time was right to broach the subject.

It had been two months since they started dating, and even though the mysteries about Sylvio remained, he gave her no other reason to keep their relationship under wraps. Sylvio had been patient with her from day one, going at her pace, and slowly she could feel her heart opening again. Every time she looked into his eyes; she was certain his heart was opening to her too. Falyn finally decided to put her worries and inhibitions aside and make her relationship with Sylvio known, starting with the rehearsal dinner and subsequent wedding of long-time family friend, Kolt Donahue.

Falyn nervously prepared the dinner with Sylvio by her side, trying not to think about everyone's opinions once the cat was out of the bag about their relationship. Besides, it was hard not to let Sylvio's strong presence at her side distract her from her thoughts. Catching him in her peripheral vision, smartly dressed in black dress pants and a blue button-up dress shirt that barely contained his impressive physique and brought out the blue in his eyes, he had stepped it up for tonight, and she was thoroughly impressed by how nicely he cleaned up. Even with his polished appearance, with his sleeves rolled up showing off his colorful collection of tattoos, and his sexily disheveled hair, he still looked like her hot motorcycle-driving boyfriend, which she appreciated.

"You look gorgeous tonight," he said, pausing in his chopping to let his eyes drift up and down her body, in the slow, sultry way he did. She had opted for a simple navy wrap dress that sat just above her knee and featured delicately braided straps that showed off her toned arms and a tasteful amount of cleavage as well as her petite hourglass figure. It was a dress that made her feel both sexy and sophisticated.

"Thank you," she said, looking down at herself, her chef's coat covering the top of the dress as they cooked. "I honestly don't know why I'm so nervous."

"This is your first big event here at Prairie Charm. I'd be nervous too if I were you," he replied with a shrug.

"It's not just that," she said, meeting his gaze. "It's just debuting our relationship to my family and friends makes me anxious. I know some have figured it out, but my parents haven't, and I don't want them to pass judgement on us, you know?"

"Do you mean over our age difference?" he asked, furrowing his brows.

"That and I don't know..." she trailed off.

"You think they'll take one look at me and label me as bad news," he chuckled, his eyes full of mirth.

"I know it's kind of funny, but yes," she said, shaking her head and letting out a nervous laugh.

"It won't be the first time, Falyn," he said. "But if people get to know me, they find out I'm more than a tattooed badass who drives a motorcycle."

Falyn turned and walked her fingers over his tattooed forearms and up over his broad shoulders. "I happen to find everything about you incredibly sexy. This body..." she said, sucking in a breath. "And your mind."

"What are the chances of someone coming into the kitchen right now?" he asked, backing her towards a part of the counter that was clear and caging her in with his towering frame.

"Pretty good," she replied. "The guests should be arriving anytime."

Sylvio frowned and leaned in, grazing his teeth over her earlobe, then whispering. "Later."

Falyn's head turned towards the door as she heard voices in the dining room and breathlessly conceded, "I think they're starting to arrive."

Sylvio stepped away to wash his hands as Falyn did the

same, unbuttoned her chef's coat, hung it up and took his hand in hers. With one deep, calming breath, they walked out of the kitchen together as a couple for the first time.

* * *

THE DELICIOUS DINNER was a resounding success. Falyn treated guests to bright and crisp summer salads, filet mignon smothered in garlic herb butter, rosemary roasted potatoes, fresh farm green beans, and for dessert, Sylvio's mother's tiramisu. As the guests cast aside their plates with satisfied smiles on their faces, Sylvio rose from the table, helping Falyn gather the dishes and bring them into the kitchen. Falyn was busy stacking dishes into the commercial dishwasher when he came up behind her and placed his hands on her hips. She leaned back against him, melting into his body as she let out a long exhale.

"Angel, that meal was incredible. You get off your feet and go visit with the guests. I'll take care of the dishes."

"Are you sure?" she asked, her eyebrows raised in question as she turned around in his arms, went on her tiptoes and hooked her hands behind his neck.

"Yes," he replied, reaching up to tuck a curl behind her ear as his fingers trailed down the silhouette of her chin. "You go back to the dining room and let me take care of this. I'll join you as soon as I'm done." With that he leaned down and captured her lips in a sweet and tender kiss.

Pulling away, she met his gaze with gratitude as she mouthed "Thank you," and exited through the swinging kitchen door.

Setting to work, cleaning the kitchen, his thoughts drifted to earlier when she officially introduced him to her parents as her boyfriend. Although he had met Duncan and Dorothy Isley at the grand opening brunch, her father, expectedly, surveyed him, his scrutiny clear. It only took one look to realize that, according to her father, no one was good enough for his daughter. Their closeness was something Sylvio picked up on immediately. Falyn's father, although visibly inspecting him, said very little, but it was her mother, a sweet, petite woman with curly snow-white hair and deep smile lines on her lovely face, that appeared to be the most judgmental. Sylvio shook his head. *It wasn't the first time, and it certainly won't be the last.*

Kitchen spotless, Sylvio rejoined the guests in the dining room, many of whom had wandered into the Great Room or outside onto the patio and grounds. Sylvio glanced over to the corner where he noticed Falyn and her mother in what appeared to be a rather animated conversation. Even from a distance he could see the look of concern etched on her mother's face and the disappointed look covering Falyn's. She had a red flush creeping up her neck, and anyone could see the conversation was a heated one.

"Hey, Sylvio." Brooks said, sidling up to him. "So, you and my sister are finally out in the open now?"

"Yeah," he replied, offering him a grin which morphed quickly into a frown as he gestured over to Falyn and her mother. "Is everything okay over there? Does Falyn need rescuing?"

Brooks chuckled and shook his head. "Best not to. My mom is the sweetest, but she always has an opinion. She'll get over it and I'll vouch for you," he added, giving Sylvio a nudge in the side.

"I appreciate it," Sylvio replied as Jane walked over holding her infant son, Gatton.

Jane smiled and looked up at Sylvio. "Falyn said you helped her prepare dinner, and that the dessert was your mother's recipe. It was so delicious. Thank you for all your help in making this dinner so special."

"My pleasure." He replied, then leaned down to look at the baby on Jane's shoulder. "That's a cute little guy you have there."

"Thank you," she said, smoothing a hand over his little head and resting it on his back. "Sorry if this is too much information, but I really need to go pump and I don't know where Emmaline went and Kolt is outside somewhere with Georgie and Thatcher. I'd ask Dorothy or Falyn, but I'm not sure I want to interrupt the conversation over there," she said, wincing and pointing a thumb in their direction, then turning back to the men, her eyes imploring. "Could one of you hold Gatton while I..."

Sylvio, without hesitation, gestured for her to hand over the baby. "I'm happy to hold him, Jane. You take your time and do what you need to do."

Jane gave him a grateful look as she carefully handed Gatton over to Sylvio and placed a spit cloth over his shoulder. Sylvio placed the baby carefully on his shoulder as Jane scurried off and Brooks excused himself, spotting Georgie. Sylvio leaned in, inhaling deeply the sweet powder smell of the infant's soft little head. He was so tiny and precious, and although he had held many babies in his time, something about holding this little one right now brought on a sort of fever he hadn't felt in years. Having a family had always been on his radar, something he wanted and hoped for in his life. When he and Charity were married, they talked at length about starting a family and even made plans to spend their first two years just the two of them, then start trying. They followed their plan, but month after month the tests came back negative. They tried for two years, and finally Charity gave up, frustrated and disappointed. He hoped she would eventually change her mind, but she hadn't, at least not while with him. Sylvio sucked in a breath; the memory of that painful time and the irony of it all was something he didn't want to think about. Not now, not here at this celebration and holding this beautiful baby boy.

* * *

FALYN WALKED AWAY from her mom, frustrated with her and her uncalled-for opinions. As soon as she asked how old Sylvio was, she could see the wariness in her eyes. As their discussion heated, Falyn reminded her that her best friend, Kolt's mother, Emmaline was married to a man 20 years her senior, that she should keep her opinions to herself and perhaps get to know Sylvio before she voiced any more of her thoughts. That seemed to shut her up and gave Falyn the opportunity to walk away. When she turned from her conversation with her mother, she was surprised to see Sylvio holding Kolt and Jane's infant son, and she could have sworn her ovaries swooned at the sight. Was there anything sexier than a tough-looking man holding a teeny-tiny baby? Someone so small and fragile in the arms of someone so big and strong. Falyn's heart fluttered as she approached them.

"Hi," she said, her eyes zoned in on the sweet baby for a moment before letting her gaze slowly drift up to meet his. The unmistakable feeling of longing filled her chest, and Sylvio surveyed her carefully, his eyes narrowing ever so slightly. *I want to have a baby.* They had only been dating a few months, and never once did it come up in conversation. Mind you, they hadn't really talked about the future, both seeming to silently agree that it was too soon. *But is it too soon? Should they be discussing the possibilities? Sylvio was significantly older than her and didn't have children, so did he want them or not?*

"You like babies?" she inquired, trying to mask the intention behind her question.

"Sure," he replied, his eyes gazing upon the infant, a sweet smile on his face. "I mean, seriously, who wouldn't like this little fella?"

"Not all men do…like babies, that is," Falyn replied, looking away, her gaze slowly coming back to meet his eyes. "My ex was emphatic that babies were not part of the picture."

"Is that something that you want?"

"Very much," she replied. "I've always pictured myself as a mom. What about you? Fatherhood ever on the agenda?"

"It once was. But as I got older, I sort of gave up on the idea," he replied honestly, looking down at the sleeping infant on his shoulder. Falyn's heart sank with his admission. "I might, however, consider the possibility again. With the right person."

An inexplicable hope filled Falyn's chest and a slow smile curved her lips as she took in his words. *It wasn't a no.*

"You'd trade in the motorcycle for a minivan?" she asked cheekily, cocking an eyebrow at him.

"Now let's not go that far," he laughed, the rise and fall of his chest making Gatton stir and scrunch up his cute little face.

Falyn leaned in, stroking the infant's head as her eyes met Sylvio's. That familiar sadness she saw before was there in the depths of his gaze, and it made her wonder if he mourned not having that life with his ex-wife. That made her stomach bottom out. It was clear to Falyn that he still loved his ex and would always have a piece of his heart reserved for her, but what wasn't adding up was the course of events. *How can he still carry feelings for someone that hurt him so badly?*

* * *

THE PARTY LINGERED UNTIL LATE, guests inside and outside, and all rooms at the bed and breakfast booked for the wedding weekend. Falyn was busy finishing cleanup inside so she asked if Sylvio could inspect the grounds to ensure nothing was left outside. Obliging, he made his way outside to see a young man in a black cowboy hat close to Falyn's cottage standing beside his Harley. Sylvio approached and immediately recognized him as part of the wedding party, Kolt's friend, Thatcher Stevens, a fellow rodeo star from Alberta.

"Hey there, Thatcher," he said, coming into the light above the garage. "Are you a fan of motorcycles?"

Thatcher glanced over his shoulder at him, his steely eyes shining, and his lips curled up in a cocky smile as he answered, "Kind of. My dad is a big motorcycle guy, but I prefer a horse."

Sylvio chuckled; this young man was as country as it got. "Does your dad still ride?"

"Yep, he used to have a Harley Davidson Fat Boy but now he rides a Road King," he replied. "My mom hates it, but he says Harleys are in his blood."

Sylvio immediately thought about his brother Antonio and how he would say something similar. *Once you drive a Harley, it becomes a part of you; it runs in your veins.* "My brother used to drive a Fat Boy too. Definitely a popular model," he replied.

They chatted a while, Thatcher sharing about the first time his dad gave him a ride on his bike, and both men admiring his classic FX Super Glide model. Sylvio immediately liked Thatcher, and something in the way he talked seemed familiar, like they had met before. *Had he been by The Pickled Pig when he was in St. Augustine for the rodeo?* Many of the young bucks liked to come by for a drink after riding broncos, or wrestling bulls, or whatever they did at those things. Sylvio had never actually been to a rodeo but had enjoyed many a conversation with a young cowboy over the years.

"It's been nice chatting with you," Thatcher said, putting out his hand to Sylvio.

They shook hands, and Thatcher walked away, heading back to his room at the guest house. Sylvio left smiling at the pleasant conversation he shared with the confident young man. Falyn exited the guesthouse, offering Thatcher a passing smile and walking towards Sylvio. He put his arms out to her, and she walked right into them, finding her place in the groove of his broad chest. Exactly where he always wanted her to be.

* * *

WEDDINGS WERE FALYN'S WEAKNESS. The thought of a new beginning and two people hopelessly in love with each other got her every time. Sitting next to Sylvio, his hand in hers, they watched as Kolt and Jane delivered beautiful vows, and when Kolt dipped Jane in front of all their guests for their first kiss, those inevitable tears pricked her eyes. Sylvio silently, without even turning to see her emotion, handed her a handkerchief from his pocket. Dabbing at her tears, she watched as Kolt and Jane rode off across their meadow on horseback into the sunset. *Will I ever find that? Someone who wants to experience every sunset with me.* A deep, cavernous ache bore into her chest as doubt crept in.

Last night, Falyn struggled to sleep; each time closing her eyes and seeing Sylvio's face, the look of guilt, sadness, and remorse in his eyes. Deep down she knew it was her subconscious playing tricks on her, but she had seen it and there was some truth to her trepidation. The more she pictured her future, the image blurred, and she wasn't sure if she was heading down another path that was going to lead to heartbreak.

Falyn peeled her hand from Sylvio's as they rose from

the bench along with the other guests exiting the ceremony site to find their cars and head over to the reception at Donahue Farms. Falyn could feel Sylvio, his warm presence behind her and his hand resting gently on the small of her back. She couldn't look at him, not now when doubt and questions kept swirling in her head. Seeing two people so hopelessly in love with each other was just a reminder of all she wanted so desperately to have for herself, and with the mysteries still surrounding Sylvio, she wasn't sure if he would ever be able to give her what she wanted. *Can I continue with that kind of uncertainty?*

They ate, they danced, the night a blur as her overactive mind edged with fog all night. Sylvio stayed with her, the perfect, attentive boyfriend. Doting on her every whim. He was a sweet man, and she adored him. Truthfully, she was finding herself falling for him. Despite all of this, he scared her. Made her question her own judgement, and she wasn't about to be duped a second time.

At the reception, they sat side by side at the table; him nursing a Coca Cola and her picking at a piece of wedding cake, looking out over the guests dancing and celebrating with the happy couple. All the warring thoughts and emotions that had been running through Falyn's head wanted to spill out of her mouth. *What does Sylvio see for his future? Am I in it? And if I am, does he want the same things I do? The marriage. The family.* Between the ceremony, seeing him the day before holding a baby, and their brief yet non-committal conversation about the future, all of it was messing with her head. Even though they had only dated a few months, she needed to know where this was going. She wasn't going to date without an endgame in mind. She was getting older, and she could already feel her biological clock ticking. She wasn't about to waste her time dating someone that she couldn't see a clear future with. Even more importantly, with someone that couldn't see a clear future with her. Even if the sex was mind-blowing, it wasn't enough to sustain a solid, committed relationship.

Analyzing how to approach the conversation, Falyn decided her first course of action needed to be asking directly about his relationship with his ex; otherwise, there was no way she could even begin to picture her future with him. Especially if he was harboring some unresolved feelings.

Falyn was tense and kept fidgeting, not sure how to start the conversation.

"Is something bothering you?" Sylvio asked, resting his hand on her thigh. "You've been off since the ceremony and I might be wrong, but I sense a heavy conversation."

She turned to face him, opened her mouth, closed it and then opened it again, blurting out. "I want to know more about your ex-wife." *Seriously, Falyn. Super smooth.*

"What do you want to know?" he asked, with brows drawn together as he leaned forward on the table and folded his hands in front of him, his gaze never leaving hers.

She gulped down hard. *It's now or never.* "Every time you share about her you have this melancholy look, that is sad and almost sorrowful. Not like someone who's been cheated on and betrayed, but like someone who continues to grieve the relationship," she said, meeting his gaze. "It's like you still have feelings for her and aren't able to let them go."

Sylvio blinked at her a few times and turned his gaze away, looking down at his hands, his mouth in a straight line, his expression stoic.

"I mean, if you still love her, what are you doing with me?" Falyn asked, desperately needing a clarifying answer.

His steely eyes flitted to hers, pinning her gaze, and his brows furrowed. "Do you really think I would start a relationship with you, Falyn, while I was still in love with my ex-wife?"

"I don't know," she shrugged ambiguously. "I didn't think my ex-husband would start relationships with other women while we were married, and well, that didn't stop him."

"Are you seriously comparing me to your lying, cheating asshole of an ex-husband?" Sylvio asked, disbelief washing over his face. "Because if you think that's who I am, then what are we doing here, Falyn?"

"I don't know Sylvio," she answered truthfully, frustration and disappointment creeping in at a rapid pace as she raised her chin defiantly. "What are we doing here? Because I can't waste my time dating someone that can't see a future with me."

"Is that what this insane conversation is all about? The future? We've only been dating for two months, Falyn. Two months. I care deeply for you, but I'm not thinking about forever yet. Not right now," he answered, folding his arms over his chest.

"Well then, I don't know if this..." she said, pointing between the two of them. "...is worth it."

Sylvio shook his head and let out an incredulous laugh, then got up from the table and glared down at her, his eyes edged with frustration, disappointment and disbelief. "I really like you, Falyn. You're beautiful, smart, so incredibly talented it literally blows my mind. But you're also stubborn, a chronic overthinker, and insecure. I fully understand why you're insecure considering what you've been through, but what I don't understand is why you're insecure with me. I've never given you a reason to be. I have been good to you. I've treated you with care and respect and cherished you," Sylvio stammered, his voice thick with emotion as he glanced away, taking a deep breath and letting it out slowly before his tortured gaze fell back on her as he continued with defeat in his tone. "I've given you a piece of myself I had locked up in a box for the last twenty-five years. A piece I thought I would never give someone again. A piece I thought I'd lost." Falyn went to speak, but he raised his hand, halting her words before they could come out. "I'm going to go get some fresh air. Come find me when you're ready to go home."

And with that Sylvio turned, walked out of the tent and into the prairie night, leaving Falyn speechless.

CHAPTER 9

ne year later

The Pickled Pig was packed for a Friday night, patrons wall to wall. Young rodeo bucks with their cowboy hats, polished up boots and fancy buckles. Pretty young things in far too little clothing fawning all over them. Rodeo weekend in St. Augustine was always a busy one.

Sylvio looked out over the crowd, his mood disintegrating by the minute. He didn't want to be here. The energy, the music, all the things he usually loved about his place were simply too much for him tonight. He was in a funk. A funk he hadn't been able to shake for far too long.

Blonde curls caught his eye, his shoulders straightened as he tried to glance over the crowd. *Falyn.* She was still occupying his thoughts a year later. The woman across the room turned, blue eyes and brightly painted red lips meeting his gaze. His heart fell to the pit of his stomach, and his shoulders sagged. *Why do I still miss her so much?* The last time he saw her was in the rearview mirror of his motorcycle while she stood on her porch, her big brown eyes sad, her arms wrapped around herself in a hug under the porch light. That was the night Falyn gave up on trying to make their relationship work and delivered a sucker punch of an ultimatum. The image of her disappointment was still burnt into his brain, causing a painful ache to clutch his heart. *I need to get out of here.*

"I'm going to cut out early," he shouted to his head bartender as he hung up a bar towel, weaved his way out from behind the bar and exited through an employee-only door, making his way to his office. Inside he slipped on his leather jacket, grabbed his bike keys and helmet and exited out the back door. Outside, the warm summer night and now muted music and chatter from inside, instantly brought a sense of calm as Sylvio took a deep breath, letting it out slowly. He was going to put his feet up and chill tonight, maybe order a pizza and watch Roadhouse. *Bad idea.* All he had to do was think of his favorite movie and the image of Falyn, writhing on his lap, her beautiful breasts bouncing as she rubbed against him shamelessly, came back like a monster truck threatening to crush him. Just the thought of her made him rock hard and ache painfully in his chest. A lethal combination.

Straddling his bike, he went to put on his helmet when he heard a voice shout his name.

"Sylvio!"

Sylvio glanced to the side to see the silhouette of a

man in a cowboy hat, and as the man approached, coming into the light, he recognized him as none other than the young cowboy he met at the Donahue wedding, Thatcher Stevens.

"I thought that was you," Thatcher said, putting out his hand to Sylvio. Sylvio took his hand, his helmet tucked under his arm. "Do you work here?" Thatcher asked, his eyes drifting over to the building and back to meet Sylvio's gaze. *Seriously, why does this kid look so familiar to me?*

"I own The Pickled Pig," he answered. "This is my bar."

Thatcher nodded his head, looking impressed, and then flashed him a puzzled look. "Why did I think you were one of the owners of Prairie Charm Bed and Breakfast? I thought maybe you owned it with Brooks' sister, Falyn?"

Sylvio's stomach dropped at the sound of her name, and he let out a sharp breath as he answered. "She owns the bed and breakfast, and we were dating."

"Were?"

"Yeah, we broke up right after Kolt's wedding." Sylvio replied matter of fact.

Thatcher lifted his hat off his head and ran his hand through his hair. "Damn, Sylvio, I'm sorry. You two looked happy," he said, giving him an empathetic look which quickly morphed into appreciation. "She sure can cook. That may have been one of the best meals I've ever had." A smile tugged at Sylvio's lips at the memory. "I'm staying there this weekend, and my parents came out to see me compete this year so they're staying there too. I was kind of hoping you'd be there so I could show my dad this beauty," he said, running his hand over the handlebars of Sylvio's Harley. "I'm sure he'd love to see this classic."

"How long are you in town?" Sylvio asked.

"We leave Monday."

"Well then, why don't you come by the bar Sunday afternoon?" Sylvio suggested, nodding over to the back exit of the bar. "I'll be working in my office, and if you knock on the back door, I'll hear it."

"Fantastic," Thatcher said, shaking his hand again and tipping his hat to Sylvio. "See you Sunday."

FALYN FLIPPED the radio station to find another song as she cruised down the highway towards St. Augustine. *Stupid love songs. Every sappy one, either about true love or hearts being broken.* Falyn didn't want a reminder of how pathetic her love life was. It had been a year since she and Sylvio broke up, and she had yet to dip her toe back into the dating pool. Truth was she wasn't sure she wanted to. It wouldn't be fair to anyone she dated as she had no doubt that she would compare them to him. He had set the bar high.

Falyn shook her head, trying to dispel the memory of the rumble of his motorcycle fading away into the night. She had approached her relationship with Sylvio so wrong. Overthinking and setting expectations that were premature and unnecessary. Scared to let their relationship grow and take its natural course. Trying to speed up the process.

Falyn had been thinking about Sylvio a lot lately. Days alone, questioning. *If I hadn't let my insecurities get the better of me, would we still be together?* Nights alone, missing the tenderness of his touch. Sylvio had been wonderful to her during their brief relationship, and she messed it up royally. If she could go back, she would, but now it was too late. As the months passed, so did the silence, and now a year later, Falyn was certain he had all but forgotten about her and moved on. *Had I even given him anything to remember?*

Falyn's car started to sputter, and she groaned. Her loaner vehicle was on its last leg. All things considered, it had done her well, but alas, she was sure as she saw the steam rise from under the hood that this was finally it. It was giving up the ghost. Pulling over to the side of the highway, the car sputtered as she cut the engine, and a final puff of steam wafted from the hood. Falyn let out an exasperated sigh, closed her eyes, and rested her head on the steering wheel in defeat. *Fuck my life.*

Falyn sat there a long time, trying to piece together her thoughts and confusing emotions. Her mind a jumble of frustration, both with the car, herself and her heart feeling cracked and bruised. Self-sabotaging wounds she didn't know how to heal from. She wasn't sure how long she sat there, the heat and humidity of the hot summer day causing a sheen of sweat to form on her skin. Staring blankly down the highway, vehicles passed her, shaking the car with each pass as she stewed in her thoughts. Suddenly, the loud, familiar rumble of a motorcycle sounded, and Falyn's eyes hazily focused on the image in her rear-view mirror. There behind her, a familiar black

Harley veered off the highway and stopped, kicking up a cloud of dust. A tall, broad man took off his helmet, his eyes covered with aviator sunglasses, messy salt and pepper hair gracing his head and dressed in a white t-shirt and tight blue jeans as he climbed off his bike. *Is this a mirage? Has the summer heat caused me to hallucinate?* The tap of knuckles on her window made her jump, and she rolled down her window. Sylvio leaned in, lifted his sunglasses and met her gaze with his beautiful blue-grey eyes. *Those eyes. God, how I missed those eyes.*

"We have to stop meeting like this," he said, the deep timbre of his voice so welcome to her ears as his mouth curved up slowly into a smile. *He's so handsome.* Her heart tightened painfully in her chest at the sight of him, his words to her at the wedding still echoing in her head. A sudden flood of emotion rose in her chest, and she blinked, hot tears pricking her eyes. Desperately she tried to hold them back, blinking rapidly now to push them away, but those big, fat, regretful tears spilled onto her cheeks.

"Are you okay?" Sylvio asked, opening her car door and crouching down to her level to cup her face, his thumbs wiping back the sudden cascade of tears.

Falyn took in a stuttering breath, and with a dry mouth choked out. "I've missed you."

His steely eyes turned from worry to tenderness as he replied, "I've missed you too, Angel." Pulling her into him, he wrapped his strong arms around her, and she drew in a strained breath, melting into the instant comfort of his arms. A place she had missed. A place she belonged. That soothing smell of his cologne, the scratch of his stubble on her cheek, the feel of his protective arms cradling her, causing her body to sigh. Releasing their embrace, he unbuckled her, rose to his feet, took her hand and pulled her out of the car. Wrapping his arms around her, he glanced at her sad-sack vehicle and a low chuckle rumbled from deep in his throat.

"What's wrong with this hunk of junk now?" he asked, his voice playful yet compassionate.

Falyn looked up at him and replied, her voice tiny and hollow, "I think it's dead."

Sylvio let out a bountiful laugh, his deep chuckle making her start to laugh too, her tears now full of irony at the situation. This damn vehicle brought them together the first time and now again. Falyn shook her head at the happenstance.

"Who's watching the bed and breakfast?" Sylvio asked curiously, looking down at her.

"My mom and Emmaline Donahue." She replied. "I was going to run some errands and well then this happened." She added, gesturing to the car.

"I'll call the tow truck, and if you don't have to rush back, I want to take you somewhere."

"Okay," she agreed. Honestly, she would go anywhere with Sylvio. She was just so happy to see him, and they needed to talk. Desperately. Whether the outcome was good or bad, there were so many things left unsaid when they broke up.

Sylvio contacted the towing company, requesting that they hold on to her vehicle until later in the day when they could come by, settle any costs and decide what to do with it.

Then, taking her hand, he led her to his bike and handed her a bottle of water from his leather bag. She uncapped it, taking a long pull of the liquid, as he brushed the damp curls from her face and tucked them behind her ear.

"Better?" he asked softly, his eyes searching hers.

"Yes."

He turned and unstrapped the extra helmet he carried from his bike and handed it to her, watching as she put it on. He leaned in, his hot breath feathering over her skin, making her eyelashes flutter as he snapped it securely under her chin. Warm, kind eyes met hers as he said. "It's not far."

SYLVIO WASN'T GOING to squander this serendipitous opportunity. Falyn had been consuming his thoughts, and as if the universe was listening, she manifested on the side of the road. As soon as he saw her car, he didn't hesitate to stop, no matter what her reaction to seeing him again would be. Then, seeing her in her sweltering car, looking so morose, her tears flowing onto her cheeks at the sight of him, well, that did him in. Every emotion that flowed out of her mirrored the regret and pain he couldn't shake since their split. He wanted her. Needed her in his life. He knew that now. It was time to let her in fully. To stop holding back his past, no matter how painful. The only way was to take her there. To a place where he could explain everything. If he wanted a fighting chance to make a relationship with Falyn work, she needed to know and understand where he'd been and what he'd been through. Something he should have done when they were together and later regretted.

They drove a mile down the highway, just outside of St. Augustine, and turned onto a country road. The gravel pulled at the tires, but he slowed, not wanting to kick up the sharp rocks. The property neared, and he turned down the long driveway he had driven down more times than he could count; the yard site treed in and not visible from the road. When they got to the yard, the bungalow house appeared with its chipped white paint and overgrown flower bed, now full of a combination of tall weeds and wildflowers. An ironic depiction of his life here. Across the yard were two large metal buildings with overhead doors and a sign above saying, "Conti Customs." The location of his once thriving motorcycle custom and repair shop. Between the business and the house was a small, one-car garage, dilapidated and leaning precariously as if one strong gust of wind would bring it to the ground. It took everything in Sylvio not to stare at the little garage, the memories pulling him in as they came flooding back. Yet there was a reason he was here again and forcing himself to relive the past. And that reason was Falyn. She needed and deserved to know about his past, no matter how painful it was going to be for him.

He parked in the middle, between the house and the shop, facing the garage. Cutting the engine and taking a moment to glance around the familiar yard site, Falyn got off the bike first and took off her helmet. Sylvio followed suit and reached for Falyn's hand, lacing his fingers with hers.

"Is this where you live?" she asked, glancing around and raising a curious eyebrow.

"No. Well, I own the property but no, I don't live here anymore," he replied. "This is where I lived when I was married, and this is the old custom bike shop I told you about. My first business." He said, pointing towards the sign above the overhead steel door. "I ran this place with my younger brother, Antonio." Falyn nodded, listening intently, giving his hand a supportive squeeze which urged him to continue.

Sylvio took a deep, calming breath and let it out slowly before he went on. "I met my ex-wife, Charity, when I was 22 at a bike rally just north of Winnipeg. She was 18, beautiful, free-spirited, super passionate, and when we met, I was instantly head over heels for her. She was a bit of a wanderer, with no family to speak of as she aged out of the foster care system and was now on her own. I felt like her hero, bringing her here to this property I purchased from my grandparents and putting a roof over her head. We were married within a few months and as far as I knew she was happy." Sylvio shared a faint smile on his lips. "We were happy."

Swallowing down hard, Sylvio could feel a bead of sweat trickle down the side of his face. *Or is that a tear on my cheek?* The part of his story he dreaded was in front of him. "I had gone on a road trip to pick up a part we needed for one of our custom jobs and planned to be back later in the day. The pickup went quickly, and I was eager to get home to Charity and to let Antonio know that we could complete another profitable job," he explained. "I got home earlier than expected and saw Antonio's truck in the driveway, which wasn't unexpected as he often worked late, and the garage door was open with Charity's little car inside. I went inside the house, seeing my brother's coveralls hung up on the hook by the door, which I thought was strange, but maybe Charity needed his help with something or perhaps she invited him inside for dinner, which wasn't uncommon. The house was all but quiet until I heard noises coming from the back of the house. As I neared the bedrooms, I heard them." Falyn's eyes grew wide, her brows drawing together as he went on. "They had been having an affair for a month, and shortly after I caught them in the act, she found out she was pregnant and left me to be with him."

Falyn curled her arm around his waist and rested her head on his chest. "Sylvio, I'm so sorry."

He squeezed her, appreciating her compassion. The tumultuousness of that time crept in slowly as the darkest of those memories came back like a Mack truck with no brakes, running right over his heart. "To make a long story short, my brother and I stopped talking, our custom bike business went bankrupt, Charity filed for divorce, and they had a baby boy."

"Were you and your brother close before all this happened?" Falyn asked.

"Best friends. He was my ride or die," Sylvio replied, taking a deep breath and letting it out slowly. "I lost my wife, my business, and my best friend and brother. Needless to say, I hit rock bottom."

Falyn nodded with understanding as she asked, "Where are they now?"

"Antonio moved away and Charity..." he started,

closing his eyes, his voice edging a tremor. "Charity committed suicide."

"Oh, dear God," Falyn gasped, bringing her hand to her mouth as she followed his gaze to the little detached garage in front of them.

"She must have come here in the middle of the night, gone into the garage and started my truck. I was asleep and never heard the truck running. She died from carbon monoxide poisoning." Falyn blinked, tears glistening in her eyes, as her gaze met his. "I'm the one who found her."

"Oh, Sylvio," she said, burying her face in his chest. "I can't imagine how awful that was."

Sylvio wrapped his arms around Falyn in a hug, swallowing back tears that threatened to escape as he continued. "For many years I blamed myself, asking why I left my keys in the vehicle, and I became angry at myself for not being a good enough husband to her." Falyn looked up at him, compassion in her gaze. "I still don't have answers as to why she did it and why she came here to do it. Part of me thinks she felt guilty about betraying me, about playing a part in pulling apart my family and my business, but honestly, I'll never know. Speculating the reason still haunts me, and I still experience nightmares about finding her."

Sylvio and Falyn stood there a long time, wrapped in each other's arms with a sorrowful silence falling on them. Finally, Sylvio reached up and caressed her face, her eyes lifting to meet his. "That's why when I talked about Charity, you saw sadness in my eyes. Despite all her transgressions, losing the one and only woman I ever loved was something that broke me worse than the cheating, worse than the loss of my business. I fell into a deep depression, and by the time I emerged, Antonio and his son were gone. He broke all contact with family and literally disappeared."

"I get it now," Falyn said simply, her eyes full of compassion and regret of her own. "I'm so sorry for what I said at Kolt's wedding and for throwing an ultimatum at you. It was so unfair of me to compare you to my ex-husband. You're nothing like him and never were. You, Sylvio Conti, are a good man and I have regretted what I said to you every day since you rode away."

"I regret not sharing all of this with you sooner," he answered, his voice shaky as tears glossed over his eyes. "It's just too hard to relive."

Falyn touched his face, smoothing her hand up over his stubbled chin and up to his hair, her hands threading through it. "Thank you for letting me in and trusting me with this. I understand now why it was hard to open up to me. Again, I'm so sorry and I've missed you, Sylvio, so much."

"I've missed you too, Falyn," he confessed, meeting her gaze. "I want to try again with you. I want to see where this goes. Getting over you…" he started, then shook his head. "…I haven't been able to get over you, Falyn. Our time together may have been brief, but you've found your way in here," he said, lifting her hand to settle it over his heart.

Falyn's expressive brown eyes glossed over with tears as she rasped out. "I want to try again, too."

Sylvio lifted her chin and leaned down, their lips an inch apart, their hot breaths mingling with the humid summer air as he searched her eyes. "I promise to take care of your heart, Falyn."

"And I promise to take care of yours," she replied as he slowly lowered his lips to hers for a tender reunion kiss. A kiss that promised they would try again, this time with no more secrets and everything out on the table.

CHAPTER 10

After leaving the property, Sylvio drove her to the garage, his mechanic confirming her car was unsalvageable. Then he brought her to his home, a cute little bungalow on the outskirts of St. Augustine, only a few miles from the bar. As he pulled into the driveway, Falyn smiled with both surprise and approval at his choice of residence. The house was pretty as a picture, a rich blue with pristine white trim. In the driveway was a two-car garage set further back which he opened with a remote from his pocket, driving his Harley inside and parking it next to a lawn mower and snowblower. On the other side sat a newer model SUV. Falyn dismounted the bike and took off the helmet as he followed, and she let out a laugh. "I thought you only drove a motorcycle." she said pointing at the SUV.

Sylvio shrugged and took off his aviators, smirking at her. "We have winters in Manitoba and how do you think I bring home groceries?"

Falyn mirrored his shrug and laughed again. This man

she thought she knew so well, not just a sexy bad ass biker but practical too.

"Let's go inside," he said, taking her hand and leading her toward the side door of his little house.

Unlocking the door, he opened it and a blast of cool air hit Falyn straight in the face. The hot humid summer day was suddenly forgotten, as Sylvio quickly shut the door behind them and led her into the kitchen. The room was small but warm and inviting with chestnut-colored butcher block countertops, white painted cabinets and dark wood handles. A little wooden table sat in the corner and two rectangular stools were tucked under the overhang of the small island occupying the middle of the room. A window over the sink framed by cheery floral curtains brought in natural sunlight as it overlooked a large fenced-in backyard. *This is not what I was expecting.* Sylvio's house, such a contrast from the edgy leather clad biker she knew. She took a seat at the island as Sylvio, dropped his keys in a bowl on the little kitchen table and rounded the island.

Falyn's eyes floated around the room, still not believing this was his place as her eyes met his. "This place is far too cute for a bad ass biker," she said aloud, echoing her thoughts.

Sylvio laughed, the deep tone of his voice making Falyn's body stir at the sound. She hadn't been with anyone since Sylvio as she wasn't sure anyone could compare. What they shared physically was passionate, raw, carnal and like nothing she had experienced before. Like their libidos matched and their bodies were simply in tune with each other. After their breakup Falyn couldn't even fathom anyone else touching her.

Sylvio opened the refrigerator and pulled out a large glass pitcher of lemonade gesturing to it, silently asking if she wanted some. Falyn nodded, a hint of mirth in her gaze as he added ice to two tall glasses and filled both up, handing one to her. She took it and raised the glass to her lips, taking a long pull of the refreshing sweet and sour liquid. Setting her glass down, she nodded her approval and swept her tongue over her lips capturing the remnants of the delicious summer drink. She should have known Sylvio would notice. His eyes immediately darkened as he swallowed. The surge of electricity that had always existed between them evidently was still there and turned all the way up.

Eyes never leaving Sylvio's, Falyn rose from her stool, taking her glass, now dripping with condensation, and rounded the island sidling up next to him. Her hand slid over his and her eyes slowly lifted to meet his lustful gaze. Reading her mind, he took her glass of lemonade and set it next to his, then in one swift move he lifted her to the countertop, her legs opening to accommodate his narrow hips and settle into the groove of her body. Biting her bottom lip, she reached for his T-shirt, pulling it forcefully from his jeans, and lifting it over his head, then off. Sylvio's body was as magnificent as she remembered, all tanned, taut muscles. Her pulse quickened as she teased and traced the edges of his abs with her fingertips and skimmed along the waistline of his jeans.

"I haven't been with anyone since you," he growled, his voice reverent. "You've ruined me woman."

Falyn smiled naughtily, leaning back on her palms, her chest heaved forward, and her head thrown back leaving her neck long and exposed. Sylvio's lips were there in an instant, kissing down the column of her neck, as one arm curled around her, supporting her back and a large palm kneaded her breast feverishly. Blazing a trail of heated kisses along her collarbone, his warm wet tongue dipping into the hollow of her throat. Falyn's breath hitched at this as her core pulsed with need for his touch.

"No one else could measure up," she rasped, as she watched him take a piece of ice from his glass and popped it into his mouth. "I haven't been with anyone since you." Sylvio grinned his approval as he took the ice between his teeth and trailed a cool wet path down between her breasts, letting it melt against her overheated skin, trails of melted water trickling down her stomach underneath her blouse. She moaned as his fingers nimbly unbuttoned her blouse. The blouse fell open, her light pink lace bra barely containing her now heaving breasts. Sliding the blouse down over her shoulders, he reached behind her and unclasped her bra, sliding it off and tossing it to the floor. His eyes dark and dilated, he reached for another piece of ice.

"You are so fucking gorgeous. I couldn't imagine touching another woman after you," he growled as he took the ice between his lips, sliding it down between her breasts and bringing it up to circle one nipple, then the other. They puckered and peaked instantly, painfully at the cool assault and Falyn cried out.

"I need your mouth on them, please."

With her plea, he ravaged her breasts, kneading, kissing, nibbling at the sensitive flesh. Drawing one nipple into his mouth, he sucked mercilessly, making her gasp. He moved onto the next giving the other side equal attention, as desire pooled between her thighs, the need for him to touch her there becoming desperate.

"Take off my shorts," she demanded as her arms gave out and she lay back, her hair drifting over the opposite edge. Doing as he was ordered he unbuttoned her shorts and shimmied them off along with her underwear leaving her bare and exposed on the cold countertop. Before she could take a breath, his hot mouth was there, devouring her center, the rasp of his tongue and rough scruff of his chin, adding to the insatiable friction. A low growl reverberated through his chest as he raised his head, his chin glistening with her intimate juices.

"I need to be inside you," he panted as he frantically fumbled with his belt, unbuttoned his jeans and slid them down mid-thigh taking his briefs along with them. Falyn lifted her head, needing to see his beautiful, engorged member, veined and throbbing to be inside her. He teased her folds with his swollen crown, making her grow impossibly wetter and then lining himself up he plunged into her. No pretense, just one carnal thrust. They let out mutual moans of gratification, the deliciously familiar fullness and exquisite stretch making her cry out his name. Giving her a moment to adjust, he began to move in and out of her slowly, deliberately, each languid thrust hitting that spot inside her that only he could reach. She tried to breathe, but it was too good, too perfect, his body playing hers with precision, taking the time to savor this reunion. Despite the cold of the room, their bodies grew hot, sticky, the smell of sweat and sex lingering in the air, as Sylvio picked up his pace, gripping her hips as he drove into her, bringing her higher with each press and pull as she wrapped her legs around his back and pressed her heels into his flexing, toned behind. Her mind in a haze of lust and desire as she neared her climax.

"Sylvio, oh God, yes," she cried out between the relentless piston of his hips.

"Look at me Angel. I need to see you come undone," he ordered, and her eyes flew open meeting him, so full of ardor. A look she had never seen before. With that her body uncoiled, all the tension and longing of the past year melting into the pleasure he was giving her. All the nights she thought of him. Missed him. Craved his touch. Suddenly a distant memory as he took her to the edge and caught her as she fell.

With one final thrust he was there with her, claiming her as his. Promising that he would never let go of her again. With chests heaving, he peeled her shuddering body from the countertop and wrapped his strong arms around her, cradling her to his chest.

Their bodies still joined, he met her satiated gaze, brushing her sweat soaked curls from her face as he kissed her languidly, his tongue teasing her to open. She tasted her arousal, their mingling sweat and the sweet taste of Sylvio on her tongue and in that moment, she knew she never wanted to be without him again. This man was hers and she, heart, mind and soul, was his.

It took all of Sylvio's willpower that afternoon to not hop on his bike and drive to Primrose to surprise Falyn at

Prairie Charm. After their sexual reunion on his kitchen countertop, they took a steamy shower together, leading to more amorous activities and eventually, they managed to leave the house. He helped her with her errands before lending her his SUV until she could get out to purchase a vehicle of her own.

Now he was here in his office at The Pickled Pig, the usually hopping bar quiet and dark on a Sunday afternoon. He liked it on days like this, when he was alone and could concentrate. Even though thinking of Falyn was seriously messing with said concentration. He shook his head and chuckled at that. Self admittedly he was a little love drunk. Their unexpected reunion, sharing his dark past and their mutual desire to give their relationship another try still felt somewhat surreal to him. Like he was going to wake from a dream. That swirling blissful feeling made his heart feel full, like a missing piece had been returned to him. The last piece of the puzzle slipping into place. This time would be different between them. Equally as passionate, but he wasn't going to hold back this time. He was going to communicate better, express and show her how special she was to him and when his heart was ready, he was going to make her his, forever. He was in love with Falyn. He was certain. Just one look into her expressive, beautiful brown eyes again and he could see his forever. *But is she in love with me?*

Sylvio honestly didn't know. She cared about him. Desired him. But did she love him? Her wounds were fresh, newer than his. He understood her not laying down her hand just yet. But if he was a betting man, he would bet his future that she loved him too.

A loud knock sounded at the back door and Sylvio glanced at his watch. 2 p.m. His brows furrowed as he rose from his desk and exited his office, headed down the short hallway to the backdoor of the club. Opening the door, Thatcher Stevens stood there, his usual black cowboy hat on and clad in his western best.

"Thatcher." Sylvio acknowledged, putting his hand out to shake. "That's right, you were going to stop by with your dad to see the bike."

Taking his offered hand, the men shook as Thatcher answered, "Sylvio, this is my father, Tony Stevens." Stepping aside, a man appeared behind him. Shorter than both Sylvio and Thatcher, his shoulders broad, and body trim and toned but not as muscular. His hair shaved short, more salt than pepper and a thick grey goatee gracing his square jaw. Sylvio squinted for a moment, their eyes meeting, the same shape and size but different colors, and the man's lips curled up into a slow smile. Sylvio blinked, sudden recognition registering as he looked beyond the age, beyond the scruff and there before him was his brother, Antonio.

"Hi, Sylvio," he said, with a wary smile. "Long time no see."

Sylvio got behind the bar as Antonio and Thatcher took a seat on stools across from him. "I can't believe you own a bar, Syl," Antonio mused. "I remember you were obsessed with that movie, Roadhouse. That one with Patrick Swayze."

Sylvio smiled, shock still radiating through him as he produced a bottle of whiskey and three glasses. He seldom drank but right now he needed a shot. Gesturing to the glasses, the men nodded, and he poured them each two fingers before returning the bottle to its perch behind the bar.

Thatcher took a sip of the straight up whiskey and winced, setting the glass down and glanced between Sylvio and his father. "So, you two know each other?"

"We do," Sylvio replied, glancing at Antonio, his eyes imploring him to explain.

Antonio slowly picked up his glass of whiskey and took a sip, then he turned to Thatcher, his hazel eyes softening as he looked at his son. "Thatcher, Sylvio is my brother..." he began. "...and your father."

CHAPTER 11

Sylvio's breath caught in his throat, and he stumbled back as if he was punched in the gut. He reached for the bar top gripping it, needing it to ground himself as Antonio's words repeated in his head. *And your father. Charity. The baby. Thatcher. Thatcher is my son. How could this be?*

Thatcher stared at the two men, his blue-grey eyes wide with disbelief as he let out a shaky laugh and said, "Dad, stop joking. That isn't funny."

Antonio shook his head, his eyes downcast. "Let me explain, son," he said looking up and glancing between the two men, Thatcher now staring blankly at his father and Sylvio barely upright, his heart pounding in his ears. "Your mother, Charity, and I had an affair, while she was still married to Sylvio." Thatcher got up from the stool and started pacing as he continued. "She became pregnant and left Sylvio to be with me. After you were born, your mother struggled. She had postpartum depression."

Sylvio's eyes darted to Antonio as he said, "I never knew that."

"I didn't either until it was too late," Antonio added, giving Sylvio a mournful look. "She was supposed to see a doctor, her hormones all out of whack after having Thatcher, and she said she made an appointment. But when I came home one night, she was bathing you…" he said, meeting Thatcher's eyes. "…and I walked in just as she slipped you under the water and held you there. I ran in, instantly pushing her out of the way and grabbing you, Thatcher. You had started turning blue but were breathing. Once I heard you cry, I wrapped you in a towel and held you tight. She never said anything, just sat there on the bathroom floor the whole time stunned as if in a haze then got to her feet, grabbed her car keys and left. That was the last time I saw her."

Thatcher took off his hat, running his hands through his dark hair, making it stand on end. Sylvio needed to sit, so he rounded the bar and took Thatcher's stool across from Antonio. Antonio slowly reached into his pocket and pulled out a piece of paper. The paper was folded in four; the edges frayed as if ripped out of a notebook as he held it out to Sylvio. Sylvio stared at the note in his outstretched hand for a moment. Without explanation knowing what this note was. *Her suicide note.* With trembling fingers, he took it from his brother's grasp. Slowly, as if it held the secrets of the world, he unfolded the paper and read:

Sylvio,

Some say true love never dies. It only gets stronger with

time. Time. I don't have that luxury it seems. I have ruined too many lives and broken too many hearts. Including my own. And I need to pay my penance. I regret so much. I regret lying to you. I regret betraying our marriage. I regret not telling you about our baby. Our baby. Thatcher is yours. I knew he was the day I left you. I was pregnant, but the damage was done. I had caused your brotherhood, your business and your heart to break. And then he was born, and I was certain. He has your eyes, Sylvio. Eyes that remind me of how much I hurt you. I don't deserve to live. To be his mother. I'm not worthy and I'm so sorry. Sorry for the pain I caused and the lies I told. I will love you Sylvio till my last breath and I hope someday you can forgive me.

Charity

Sylvio set the letter on the bar and closed his eyes, stinging tears piercing them as he took in several deep cleansing breaths. Charity's last words, ones of guilt. Words of pain. *Why wouldn't she have sought help? How did Antonio not recognize it sooner?* Sylvio let out a long exhale as a deep understanding washed over him. 25 years had passed and there would never be answers. What mattered was the here and now. *I have a son.*

Antonio handed Thatcher the letter, and he read it, shaking his head, his brows furrowing with confusion as he asked, "Why wouldn't you tell Sylvio about me?"

"I honestly didn't know myself until a few years ago." Antonio replied. "After Charity passed, I had an opportunity to go work in Alberta and took it, thinking distance from the situation would be a good idea, all things considered. You were only six months old when your mother died, and I needed to support you and myself. I settled in

Smoky Lake and a year later I met your mother. A year after that we were married, and your sister was born. It wasn't until I was going through some old boxes, things I had long forgotten about, that I found Charity's journal in one of them. I found the letter in there." Antonio shook his head, running his hands down the front of his jeans as he met Sylvio's gaze. "Trust me Syl, if I knew I wouldn't have kept him from you. When I found the letter, I wasn't sure what to do. Too much time had passed, Thatcher was an adult and you and I hadn't spoken in decades. Then Thatcher came home after Kolt Donahue's wedding, excited about this Harley he saw and this guy who owned it. I asked his name, and he said, 'Sylvio Conti.'" Antonio let out a little chuckle as his eyes drifted over to Thatcher, so much fatherly love in his gaze. "I just knew I had to find a way back to Manitoba." Antonio's eyes met Sylvio's. "I have carried the guilt of betraying you half my life and I know my actions back then aren't forgivable. But I've missed you brother. More than I can say."

With that he stood, tears in his eyes as he put his hand out to Sylvio. An olive branch. Sylvio stared at his hand a moment, his face strained, and grief stricken, but finally he stood, and he took his offered hand pulling him into an embrace. As they hugged, shoulders shaking as they cried, all the weight of anger and animosity that Sylvio carried for so long lifted and washed away like the tide. Two estranged brothers finally reunited for good.

* * *

LAYING BACK against the slope of her free-standing tub, Falyn sighed. *Best investment ever.* She had been slowly renovating her little cottage and had plans to build on, potentially adding a second floor with a bedroom or two. For now, however, expanding the bathroom to make room for this tub was by far her best decision yet. The heat of the water mixed with the lavender Epsom salts made her muscles sigh and all the wound-up tension of the weekend left her body. *Bliss.*

Sylvio had texted her earlier, saying he would come over to spend the night. She couldn't wait to see him and to have him back in her bed. After their unexpected reunion and the revelation of his past, her heart and mind were full. Full of questions, full of ideas, full of deep respect, adoration and love. She loved Sylvio. If she was being honest with herself, she had known long before. She was just too scared to admit it back then. Telling herself it was too soon, yet wanting nothing more than to speed up and make him hers forever. She was done holding back and denying herself what she clearly wanted. A committed relationship with Sylvio Conti.

The sound of the front door disengaging made her breath catch as she sank lower into the luxurious bath. He had found the key she hid for him.

"Angel. Where are you?" he called, the low timbre of his voice making her heart flutter. His head peeked into the bathroom, and he smiled that slow, sexy smile she loved so much as he slipped into the steamy room. "Or perhaps I should call you a mermaid. You look comfortable. Nice tub."

"I just put it in. It's amazing." She breathed out, pushing a wet curl from her face and cocking an eyebrow at him. "Would you like to join me? There's room for two."

Sylvio's steely eyes dilated as he made quick work of stripping off his clothes and climbing in behind her, her body cradled between his thick muscular thighs. Taking a deep cleansing breath, he leaned back, taking Falyn with him to rest on his chest and exhaled slowly. "Apparently, I don't take enough baths, as this is amazing," he said as his large palm found her breast and languidly fondled it.

Falyn giggled, as she melted into his body, and asked, "How was your day?"

"Good. I finished up some paperwork, arranged all the orders I needed to make for the week, reunited with my brother, and oh, I found out I have a son."

"What?" Falyn asked, shifting her body, to turn and face him.

He met her gaze, so much happiness in his eyes as he explained. "Thatcher Stevens is my son, and his father, Tony, is my brother Antonio."

"You mean the guests staying at Prairie Charm this weekend? That rodeo cowboy from Alberta that's friends with Kolt and Jane?"

"One and the same," he replied as his brows drew together with trepidation. "How do you feel about it? Me, having a son."

Falyn stared at him a beat and replied, "I think you need to ask yourself that question. How do you feel about it and how do you know Thatcher is your son?"

"It's a long story," he replied as she settled back into

the groove of his body, and he wrapped his arms around her. They spent the next hour talking first in the tub and then in bed, him telling her about Charity's postpartum depression, the circumstances that led to her taking her own life, the note found decades later. The plans they had made together to do a DNA test to be sure of his paternity and how they were going to have breakfast together in the morning, Antonio introducing Sylvio to his now wife Suzanne. The pure joy in his voice made her heart swell for him. He had answers. The closure he needed. He had a son. A question of her own popped into her mind but she hesitated a moment, unsure if it was a mistake to ask.

"Falyn, I feel like you have something to ask me," he said facing her, his fingers coming up to tuck a curl behind her ear. *How does he do that?*

"Now that you have a son, do you see yourself having any other children?" she asked, hoping desperately that she wouldn't open a can of worms again considering they just got back together.

Sylvio met her gaze, his eyes soft and sparking in the dim lamplight. "Falyn, my sweet angel. I want nothing more."

"But do you want them with me?" she asked, needing the validation.

"I want everything with you Falyn. Just give us time. As long as we need to strengthen us, then I promise you that I will give you all you want and more. I love you, Angel," he declared as he pulled her closer, chest to chest. "Do you want that with me?"

"More than anything." She breathed out shakily as she

reached up, caressing his face in her hands. "I love you too, Sylvio. So very much."

No more words being spoken, their declarations of love hanging in the air between them, they made love. Slowly, tenderly joining their bodies like a sealed promise of a future they dreamed of together.

CHAPTER 12

The summer heat turned to a fall chill, signifying the end of yet another summer season. Sylvio found himself spending more and more time at Prairie Charm. With a revolving door of new and interesting guests, helping Falyn in the kitchen and maintaining the grounds, wherever he was needed he jumped in and loved every minute of it. Of course, spending so much time at Prairie Charm meant seeing Falyn, his Angel, the woman he had fallen deeply in love with. As the months passed and their relationship grew stronger, he couldn't imagine being anywhere else than by her side. Through his reunion with Antonio and the discovery that he had a son, Falyn had been his rock. Supportive and encouraging, when the DNA results came in confirming his paternity, it was she that held him as he cried tears of joy. All he wanted was to spend every day and night with her, but his bar wouldn't allow it.

Sylvio had owned The Pickled Pig for 18 years. 18 years, schlepping drinks, acting as a therapist for patrons, helping his employees support themselves and their families. He had seen singers and bands like the now famous Prairie Sound grace The Pickled Pig stage. He had witnessed first kisses, declarations of love, engagements, a few marriages and more than his share of breakups. He had observed a slice of people's lives in St. Augustine and given all of himself in return. He was now ready to take back his life and walk away.

"I think I'm going to sell The Pickled Pig," he said as he climbed into bed next to Falyn. "My heart isn't in it anymore."

"And give up your *Roadhouse* dreams?" Falyn asked cheekily as she offered him a wink and patted him on the chest. "What are you going to do then?"

"What do you think about taking on a partner?" he inquired. "I could invest in Prairie Charm and maybe sell my house, as well as the country property and move in here."

"You would do that?" she asked, cocking a curious brow at him.

"Of course. I like it here." You've built something amazing, Falyn. I want to be a part of it," he replied.

"And you want to give up your cute little house to move into my little cottage?" she asked, climbing onto his lap and straddling his hips. His body responded immediately to her hovering heat.

"I want to be wherever you are, Angel. Go to bed with you every night and wake up and cook breakfast with you every morning for the guests," he replied, settling his hands on her hips.

Falyn laughed lightly, her fingertips tracing circles

through the smattering of hair on his chest. "I mean you are my best sous chef."

"These hands were meant for dicing," he said, wiggling his fingers in front of them.

"I thought they were meant for other things," she commented coquettishly as she guided his fingers between her legs.

"They are very talented fingers," he replied, breaching the panel of her underwear to find her soft and wet.

"That they are," she replied breathlessly, rocking against his hand. "Alright, you're hired."

CHRISTMAS WAS Falyn's favorite time of year. A time she could fulfill her fantasies of recreating a picturesque Hallmark worthy Christmas Inn with the gigantic tree and more green garland and red bows than you could count. Large poinsettias graced every surface, and the smell of spicy cinnamon sticks and ginger cookies filled the air. Everything about Prairie Charm oozed the country Christmas of her dreams.

"When you told me you loved Christmas, you weren't kidding," Sylvio remarked, entering the great room, his eyes drifting over the decked-out hearth of the fireplace. "And you said you were getting a tree delivered?"

"It's a big tree, so it requires a big truck," she replied, setting down a large basket of homemade ornaments. Sylvio walked over and picked up a pretty one made from dried orange slices and strung with a gold ribbon. Bringing it to his nose, he nodded in approval of the citrus scent as he set it down in the basket. "Are you excited about Antonio and his family coming for the holidays?"

A wistful smile curled his lips, and he nodded as he took a seat on the couch by the fireplace. Falyn joined him, snuggling into his side as the fire crackled lightly, a new log needing to be added. "I'm still not sure if Thatcher is coming though."

Falyn's heart ached for Sylvio. Since the revelation that Thatcher was his son, followed by the DNA confirmation, Thatcher hadn't so much as reached out to Sylvio. Antonio being his only line of communication with his son, he shared that Thatcher was struggling with the revelation, and Falyn could understand that. His perception of reality was altered in an instant. But seeing Sylvio long to get to know his son and him not respond was difficult to watch. All she could do was support him and be his listening ear. *But is that all that I can do?* She had a direct connection to his dearest friends, Kolt and Jane, and perhaps if she talked to them, they could convince Thatcher that he should come out with the rest of his family this Christmas.

* * *

FALYN PULLED up in front of the Donahue farmhouse. Kolt was out front shoveling snow off the walkway. The two-story white farmhouse with a wrap- around porch, surrounded by trees dusted with sparkling snow was as welcoming as always.

"Hey Kolt," she said as she got out of her vehicle and

rounded the front. "Is Jane around? I was hoping to talk to both of you."

Kolt's brows drew together, and a wary look covered his face. "Sounds serious!"

Falyn made her way towards him and clapped him on the back. "Not bad, I just could use your help. Let's go inside and discuss."

Kicking the snow off their boots at the door, they stepped inside and hung up their coats as a little rosy-cheeked, fair headed boy came running down the hallway, straight for Kolt.

"Daddy!" the little boy squealed as he bumped into Kolt's legs with a thud. Kolt laughed as he scooped him up, giving him a hug. Gatton Donahue was now 19 months old and the epitome of brown eyed blonde-haired cuteness.

"Hi there, my little rascal," he said affectionately as he planted scruffy kisses on his sweet cheeks, making Gatton giggle before turning to Falyn. "This is Falyn, Uncle Brooks sister."

"Uncle Brooksy!" Gatton said before he squirmed out of Kolt's hold and he set him down so he could scurry off.

Falyn let out a big laugh. "Brooks is always everyone's favorite! Speaking of Brooks and Georgie, are you waiting as anxiously as I am for them to finally set a wedding date?"

Jane piped in from the kitchen as they entered the room. "I don't think they'll wait much longer." she said as she turned off the kettle and asked. "Tea?"

"Sure," Falyn replied. "I'm honestly just happy they made it through, and Georgie is getting stronger every day. I saw her the other day, and she looked so good, more and more like her old self."

Kolt nodded in agreement gesturing for her to take a seat at the kitchen table. Jane joined them, balancing three mugs of piping hot tea and dividing them out between them. Falyn added a dollop of honey and stirred her tea watching the spoon swirl in the mug. Slowly she brought her eyes back up to meet Kolt and Jane's waiting and curious gazes.

"I was wondering if I could recruit your help?" Falyn asked, her eyes drifting between the two of them.

"Sure. What do you need help with?" Kolt asked, leaning his elbows on the table.

"I need Thatcher to come out this Christmas with the rest of his family. Ever since he found out that Sylvio is his father he hasn't reached out or responded to Sylvio and I think if I could give anything to Sylvio this Christmas it would be the gift of having his son spend the holidays with him."

"What do you want us to do?" Jane asked, lifting her mug of tea to her mouth and taking a ginger sip.

"I want you to talk to him. Maybe invite him out this way. Give him another reason to visit other than Sylvio and the fact that the rest of his family is spending the holidays in Primrose," she suggested. "I know you're close with him and maybe if we can get them in the same room and get them talking, Thatcher may see the value in getting to know Sylvio."

"I don't think he hates Sylvio in any way, I think he's just confused. Like everything you once knew is not as it seems," Kolt voiced. "But I had no idea he wasn't talking with him at all."

Falyn sighed and looked down into the darkness of her tea. "Sylvio is a good man and has such a huge heart. He has lost a lot in the past and now something good has come out of the tragedy of it all. He deserves to get to know his son."

"I agree," Jane concurred. "Speaking as someone who lost their only family in a tragic way, Thatcher is lucky to have not one but two loving fathers who want to be a part of his life. How lucky is that?"

STANDING in the parking lot next to his SUV, Sylvio stared at the FOR-SALE sign that graced the front of The Pickled Pig. *No going back now. It's time.* Hands in the pockets of his leather jacket, he rocked back and forth in his boots, thinking about who might buy the bar and whether they would keep the *Roadhouse* honky tonk vibe or turn it into some trendy night club. Whatever the case, when he handed over the keys it was their choice and he had to be okay with that. The passenger side door opened, and Falyn slid out, coming up beside him and wrapping her arm around his waist.

"I figured I'd give you a minute," she said, gently. "I know how much this place means to you."

Sylvio smiled down at her. His beautiful girlfriend, a welcome catalyst for this change in his life. Meeting her had in many ways given him his life back. He was no longer living day by day but was looking towards the future. A future with Falyn.

"I was just thinking about what the future owners might turn this place into. Will they keep it The Pickled Pig or change it to something trendy like a swanky nightclub?'

Fallon curled up her freckled nose and winced, "God forbid."

Sylvio laughed a big, bountiful laugh and pulled her in tightly, planting an affectionate kiss on her head. "Let's stop at my house and pick up the rest of my things. Maybe we'll even have time to christen the counter again in the kitchen," he said waggling his eyebrows at her.

Falyn laughed and peeled herself away from him, sauntering back to his vehicle and glancing at him over her shoulder. "Don't just stand there, you sexy bad boy. You have a lot to do."

CHAPTER 13

To say Sylvio was nervous was the understatement of the century. Antonio, his wife, Suzanne, as well as their 23-year-old daughter, Cassidy, were set to arrive any time. He hadn't seen his brother since the summer when they were reunited and spending the holiday season with family for the first time in years was something he was not only looking forward to but hadn't realized he missed so much. *If only Thatcher was with them.* After having found out that Thatcher was his son, he was hopeful for them to build a relationship, but Thatcher had been left hurt, his self-identity shattered. Understandably so, his whole world was being turned on its side. Even though his rejection hurt, Sylvio remained hopeful that someday Thatcher would come around. For now, there wasn't going to be anything that stopped him from enjoying this time with his family. A long overdue gathering for the holidays.

A van pulled into the driveway, Sylvio's eyes flitting to the window to see his brother Antonio get out of the vehicle. Eagerly he rushed to the door, Falyn following behind him. Antonio, now pulling suitcases out of the hatch of the van, turned and smiled at Sylvio as he strode over and hugged him with a firm clap on the back. Just then, Sylvio's eyes caught on a familiar black cowboy hat and his gaze met the blue-grey eyes that reflected his. *Thatcher.* Tears welled up in Sylvio's eyes as he stepped towards his son, putting his hand out to him to shake. Thatcher smiled sheepishly, tipped his hat and took his hand. Sylvio pulled him in for a hug and Thatcher exhaled against his shoulder, "Merry Christmas, Dad."

* * *

FALYN HAD NEVER SEEN Sylvio this emotional, so overcome by a mix of joy, relief and acceptance. He let the tears fall on the shoulders of his son, Thatcher doing the same, both men letting it all go, and laughing through their tears. A beautiful moment witnessed between father and son. Falyn strode down the walkway, to join them, hugging Antonio and Thatcher before moving on to his wife and daughter. Luggage retrieved, they all made their way into the guest house, where Falyn checked them in, and she and Sylvio took them to their rooms. While Sylvio talked with Antonio and Suzanne, Falyn directed Cassidy and Thatcher to their rooms down the hallway, Thatcher hanging back and turning to Falyn.

"Kolt and Jane told me you talked to them," he said, taking off his hat and running a hand through his hair. "The whole thing was so messed up, you know. It was hard to get my head around it all."

"I can understand that," she replied. "Sometimes good can come from tragic circumstances and I think both of your fathers would agree that you were the good."

Thatcher's eyes shone, as he contemplated her words, and he nodded, glancing down the hall to Antonio and Sylvio, laughing in the doorway of the master bedroom. "I think I got pretty lucky."

"Damn right you did," she agreed with a wink. "Now settle in and I heard through the grapevine that you loved my cooking so be ready for a celebration feast tonight."

Thatcher grinned and rocked in his boots as he let out a low appreciative whistle.

* * *

THEY STUMBLED across the yard towards the cottage. More like Sylvio stumbled and Falyn made sure he reached his destination safely. The night had proven to be a success with their bellies full of the delicious food and wine, their sides hurting from the laughter and their hearts full of love. Sylvio was self-admittedly not much of a drinker but tonight he let loose, and Falyn couldn't deny that she liked this relaxed side of him.

"I got the coolest kid; don't I have the coolest kid?" Sylvio asked, managing to get onto the porch, pulling Falyn along with him.

"Thatcher is pretty great," she replied, taking the house keys from his hand and unlocking the front door.

"He's a rodeo star, a lawyer, and he wants to own his own business someday, can you believe it, Falyn?" he said as he swayed his way to the couch. "He wants to be an entrepreneur like me."

"He takes after his dad, then," she replied, climbing onto his lap.

"He called me Dad," Sylvio said, his steely eyes glassy with a combination of alcohol and emotion. "I cried."

Too damn cute. Falyn laughed and ran her hands through his hair making it stand on end. He groaned in response and eased back against the corner of the couch.

"I love being a dad," he declared, his eyes locking on hers. "I want you to be a mom, Angel. Maybe we'll have a girl, with your blonde curls and brown eyes. She's going to be so pretty."

Falyn smiled as she added, "Or maybe a boy with dark hair and blue-grey eyes like Thatcher."

Sylvio nodded and flashed her his sexy grin. "I can't wait to have that with you, Angel." his eyes closing then opening slowly to half-mast. "I want to marry the heck out of you."

"Sylvio Conti, are you proposing to me?" she asked playfully knowing it was the libations talking right now.

"Not yet, but I will," he replied, a slow grin curling his lips as his eyes drifted closed. "Soon."

Falyn traced her fingertips over his eyebrows and down his masculine jaw, leaning in to plant a kiss on his lips, his mouth twitching with the brush of hers. A light rumbly snore sounded, his chest rising and falling rhythmically. *Asleep.* Falyn smiled and climbed off his lap, arranging the pillows at the headrest and gently guiding him to lay his head down. Lifting his feet onto the couch she reached for a thick throw blanket draped over the back of the couch and spread it out, covering Sylvio. Smoothing her hand over his hair she leaned down, kissed his cheek and walked to their bedroom ready to dream about weddings and babies and everything beautiful that came thereafter.

* * *

THE NEXT MORNING Sylvio left the cottage, a steaming coffee mug in hand as he squinted at the sun glistening off the snow. Falyn let him sleep in a little longer, but he made sure to be up in time for breakfast. The familiar black hat caught his eye as he saw Thatcher standing on the back patio of the guest house. Crossing the driveway, he made his way to a short path leading to the patio and Thatcher turned, offering him a smile.

"Good morning," Thatcher said, his gloved hands in the pockets of his tan sheepskin jacket. Sylvio stepped in line with him following his gaze to the edge of the tree line, covered in sparkling hoarfrost. They stood there a moment in contemplative silence, both men staring off into the distance until Thatcher broke their revery. "You know my dad was always honest about my birth mother. Dad would keep pictures of her around and never hid who she was from me even though I've always known my mom, Suzanne, to be my mom," Thatcher said, shaking his head and letting out a nervous laugh. "It's all so damn confusing."

"I know," Sylvio agreed. "You look like her though. A lot like her and little like me."

Thatcher turned to him and gave him a lopsided smile.

"I'm sorry everything happened the way it did, for you, I mean my dad, Tony lost but you lost everything. It wasn't fair. That part was hard to get my head around and I'm not sure I fully have yet."

"I don't blame your dad, not anymore. We were both young and stupid," Sylvio replied, looking towards the trees again, and Thatcher's gaze followed him as he continued. "You know they say time heals all wounds and I agree with that in many ways. It dulls the ache and eventually you go days, weeks, months and years not feeling the pain. It numbs with time. I held on to a lot of hurt and pain from my past for a long time. It had dulled, but it was never completely gone. When I read your birth mother's note to me, I finally understood. We were so young when we met and got married. I poured my heart and soul into my business and Charity often took a back seat to my obligations. When I met her, she was a bright, bold light, but also a bit of a lost soul. Looking back now, I know my neglect dimmed her light. I loved her and did my best, but I didn't know how to balance both. It played a part in her straying, and although that doesn't excuse what your father did. What they both did. It does however make so much more sense to me now."

Thatcher nodded. "Hindsight is always 20/20, isn't it?"

"Always," Sylvio agreed, a melancholy smile curling his lips. "Someday, God willing, I can be a better husband."

"Are you going to marry, Falyn?" Thatcher asked, his smile growing wide. "I like her. A little weird if she was my stepmother though as she's like only seven years older than me."

Sylvio shrugged and laughed, "What can I say, I still

got it." This made them both laugh. "How about you? Any pretty little fillies waiting for you back in Alberta?"

"I'm on the rodeo circuit. What do you think?" he asked, cocking a coy eyebrow at Sylvio.

"Ah, the buckle bunnies," Sylvio replied with a nod, slipping his arm over his son's shoulders. "As long as you wrap it before you tap it."

"Been a dad all of five minutes and you're giving me a birds and bees talk," Thatcher said with a sardonic chuckle.

They turned and walked together back to the front door of the guest house. "I've got to make up for lost time, son."

* * *

THE CHRISTMAS SEASON came and went, New Year fireworks marking the beginning of yet another year and his last as the owner of The Pickled Pig. There had only been a few lowball offers thus far, all of which Sylvio had turned down. He was aware he was being picky, but the Pig was his legacy and he wanted it to go to someone who honored that. His phone rang, and he picked it up glancing at the number. *My realtor.*

"Hey Ford."

"We got an interesting offer today," his hot shot commercial realtor informed. "20K over asking, 150K cash down payment and fully funded for the rest. The buyer wants a full legal license to the name and plans on keeping the aesthetic. Basically, other than some minor upgrades, Sylvio, he plans on keeping The Pickled Pig as is."

"Well then, bring me the paperwork. Sounds perfect. Who's the purchaser?" Sylvio asked curiously.

"Let me see here..." Sylvio could hear papers being moved around his desk. "Ah, here it is. Stevens. Thatcher Stevens."

CHAPTER 14

It had been a long day at the bed and breakfast and all Falyn wanted was a long hot bath and to curl herself around Sylvio. He had been gone most of the day, working at the Pig and she had missed him. Living with Sylvio had proven to be surprisingly easy. After her marriage ended, she had forged her own path and valued her independence. She couldn't see herself living with someone else, sharing her space or her life. Then a bad boy on a Harley rode in and changed that. *What a cliché?* Falyn chuckled to herself. Loving Sylvio had been her choice, and now all she wanted was to do life with him by her side.

Falyn heard the garage door open and close as she slipped out of her work clothes and leaned against the doorway of the bedroom in just her underwear. Sylvio was hanging up his leather jacket when his eyes caught on her from across the room.

"Well, isn't this a nice welcome home," he said, his lips lifting into a sexy smirk.

Falyn pinned him with a wanton stare and crossed her ankles casually as she took him in, powerfully framed and broad, all muscles and tight jeans. *It will never get old having him come home to me.* She bit her bottom lip the way she knew drove him wild.

Sylvio growled and stalked towards her as she squealed and turned to get away, but he caught her around the waist, lifting her and tossing her to the bed. In an instant he covered her, the warmth of his body hovering above her as he brushed the curls from her face. "Hi," he said huskily.

"Hi," she replied, pulling his t-shirt from his jeans and running her hands under his shirt, over the taut muscles of his back. "Did you have a good day?"

"I did," he replied, his smile wide. "I accepted an offer on the Pig."

"Really?" Falyn squeaked in question as her eyes grew wide.

"Yep, signed and accepted," he answered. "And you will never believe who made the offer."

"Who?"

"Thatcher."

"Are you serious?" Falyn asked. "Your son wants to buy The Pickled Pig?"

"Yes, and keep the name, the aesthetic, everything." Sylvio beamed, emotion edging his voice. "Thatcher is going to carry on my legacy."

Falyn pulled him in for a hug and rolled him over, inverting their position to straddle his hips. "Oh, my God, Sylvio! This is exactly what you wanted!" she exclaimed, leaning down and capturing his lips in a passionate kiss.

Sylvio rolled back on top of her and framed her face with his hands.

"I want to take you out tomorrow to celebrate. Do you think you could steal away?" he asked, his steely eyes twinkling in the dim lamplight.

"I don't have new guests until Wednesday; I'm all yours," she replied. "Where are you going to take me?"

A slow smile curled Thatcher's lips as he replied, "You'll see."

* * *

DRIVING UP TO ISLEY FARMSTEAD, Sylvio's heart was racing. He couldn't remember a time when he was this nervous. Getting up early and telling Falyn he had a few errands to run before their date starting that afternoon, his first order of business was talking to her parents. He had spent some time with them since he and Falyn reunited, and he moved into her cottage. Every time with Falyn there as a buffer, keeping conversation light. It didn't take a rocket scientist to figure out that they were wary of him. Honestly, he wasn't 100% sure how they felt at this point, but he was about to find out. He reached into the pocket of his leather jacket and gripped the little velvet box in his palm, the one that contained his promise of forever. Before he made any promises, he needed her parents' blessing first.

Getting out of his SUV, he took a deep breath as he looked at the modest two-story farmhouse. It was nothing fancy, but humble and friendly. Just as her parents were. No pretension, just honest to goodness, good people. He came from good people. People like the Isleys, and he wanted them to accept him as part of their family. With one last calming breath, he made his way down the snowy walkway to the front door of the house. Knocking, he waited. No answer. He knocked again.

"Is that you, Sylvio?" a deep, gruff voice asked behind him. He spun around to see Falyn's father, Duncan Isley, walking across the farmyard with a pail in his hands as he approached him.

"Hi there, Mr. Isley," Sylvio said, putting his hand up in a wave. If you looked under 'farmer' in the dictionary, Sylvio was sure Duncan's picture would be there. Dressed in insulated coveralls, tall rubber boots, and a Hastings Hardware cap on his snow-white hair, he trudged across the yard to where Sylvio stood.

"A bit early for a visit. Where's Falyn?" he asked, looking towards Sylvio's vehicle.

"She doesn't have guests for a few days, so I encouraged her to sleep in. Your daughter works too hard," Sylvio explained.

"That she does. Always has been a hard worker, that one," her father mused, a smile tugging at his lips. "Well, c'mon in, I was about to fix some breakfast," he said, holding up a pail of fresh eggs. "Dorothy is out for breakfast with the ladies this morning, so I appreciate the company."

Sylvio grinned and followed him into the house. The Isley farmhouse was modest with a small front porch, more like a mudroom where barn coats, coveralls, and boots found their home before one entered the house itself. Inside, a small entrance opened to a hallway with stairs to the bedrooms, a doorway to the eat-in kitchen, a bathroom down the hall, and finally the family room at the back of the house. The house, although small, was larger than the one Sylvio grew up in, and when he walked inside, he could almost hear the giggles of kids running up the stairs and the smell of fresh baking from the kitchen. Entering the kitchen, Duncan gestured for Sylvio to take a seat, so he slipped out of his jacket and hung it on the back of a wooden chair.

Clapping his hands together, Sylvio asked, "Can I help you with anything?"

"No, no. Pour yourself some coffee and have a seat, just going to fry us some eggs."

Sylvio nodded and opened a cupboard above the coffeepot, where the mugs were stored, and poured both he and Duncan a mug full, handing one to him. He gave him a grateful look as he pulled out a large cast-iron skillet. Sylvio took a seat, watching as he cracked farm-fresh eggs into the skillet and put bread into the toaster. Silence fell on the men, the only sound in the kitchen the sizzle from the skillet. In short order, Duncan had plated fried eggs and toast and handed a plate to Sylvio. Taking a seat across from him, the men dug into their meals, and it wasn't until Duncan set his fork down that he spoke. "So, I assume you're here to talk about Falyn."

"I am," Sylvio replied, setting his fork down as well, then lifting his mug to take a sip of the dark, bitter liquid before he got down to the purpose of his visit. "I love your daughter very much and I know that if you had a choice for Falyn, you would likely choose someone younger, perhaps even someone else. But I want you to know, I want to spend the rest of my life with her and I..."

Duncan raised his hand before he could go on with his speech. A well-rehearsed monologue he had spent all night trying to perfect so he could say all he needed to say.

Duncan cleared his throat and leaned onto the table, feathering his thick, calloused fingers before he lifted his gaze to Sylvio and responded. "As a father, you always hope your children make good choices. You pray they find their way in life and find happiness. You try to help them and shield them even though they're adults and can figure out difficult things on their own. You try to keep them from getting hurt." Sylvio nodded in response. "My daughter was deeply hurt by her ex-husband, as you know. He was a pompous, arrogant and exceedingly selfish man who tried to stifle my daughter's spirit and turn her into what he thought was acceptable. He forced her to sacrifice for him, and watching it happen while being so far away from her was hard for both Dorothy and me."

"I can understand that."

"So, then you can understand how cautious we were when she introduced you to us," he continued, pinning Sylvio with his gaze. "Like Pierre, you are a savvy business owner, older, more experienced in the ways of the world. So, at first impression, that's all we see, and we worry that Falyn will have to give up on what she wants in life all over again."

"I would never ask her to sacrifice for me, and I would never try to squash her spirit," Sylvio replied, his brows drawing together. "It's what drew her to me the first time we met. How smart and resilient she is and how she knows what she wants."

Falyn's father nodded his head. "Her ex-husband never saw that about her. You do. That's why we, my wife and I, approve of your relationship and self-admittedly feel a little sheepish that we judged you. You're a good man, Sylvio, and it is as plain as day that you love our daughter."

Sylvio's shoulders eased with his words, and a smile tugged at his lips as he took a deep breath, ready to ask the question he came here to ask. "Thank you. Last night I accepted an offer on my bar and in three months' time I will be passing on the keys to my son, Thatcher, whom you've met before. After that I will be sinking both my time and money into Prairie Charm. Anywhere Falyn is, is where I want to be, which brings me to why I paid you a visit this morning. I want nothing more than to spend my life with Falyn, to get married and have a family. To do all the things I've always wanted to do and never did. I want to see Falyn as a mother and support her in her business. To make her happy."

"You already do, Son."

Son. A simple term of endearment that brought on a lump of emotion constricting Sylvio's throat. Sylvio gave him a grateful smile as he swallowed down the last of his nervousness and asked. "Do I have your blessing to ask Falyn to be my wife? I know it's a bit old-fashioned, but it would mean a lot to me, and I know it would mean a lot to her."

Falyn's father sat back in his chair and brought his

arms back, folding his hands to cradle the back of his head as he stared toward the ceiling. Sylvio wasn't quite sure if he should say more or just wait, but her father closed his eyes and inhaled deeply, then let out a long-drawn-out exhale before his hands dropped to the table and his eyes met Sylvio's questioning gaze. Duncan's eyes were now glazed over with emotion of his own as he leaned forward and clapped Sylvio on the shoulder. "We would be honored to welcome you to our family. Yes, Son, you have our blessing."

Pure joy filled Sylvio's heart as he rose from the table, his future father-in-law following suit, and the men hugged, clapping each other on the back.

"What's all this?" the sweet voice of Dorothy Isley said from the cased opening of the kitchen. An amused grin covered her face as she took in the two men embracing, and her eyes caught on Sylvio. "Are you finally here to ask for our blessing to marry Falyn?"

Sylvio threw his head back in a laugh, Duncan joining in on the laughter as he pulled his wife in for a hug. "Nothing gets past my wife."

"Falyn's the same way," Sylvio replied with an amused smile.

"The apple doesn't fall far from the tree."

Dorothy gave her husband a playful swat on the chest as she met Sylvio's gaze. "Now tell us what you have planned. I just love a good proposal."

CHAPTER 15

Waiting for Falyn to emerge from the bedroom, Sylvio leaned against the countertop, scrolling through his phone. The offer to purchase, signed, sealed and delivered, had come through, so between messages from his realtor, messages from his lawyer and messages from Thatcher, he had been inundated all day. He appreciated the distraction, considering his morning chat with her parents and their blessing to ask Falyn to marry him. The ring was safely tucked into the inside pocket of his leather jacket ready for the right moment and although he was nervous earlier in the day, having her parents' approval eased his nerves so he could enjoy his date with Falyn that would eventually lead to him getting on one knee.

Stuffing his phone into his pocket, he looked up to see Falyn come out of the bedroom, and he couldn't help but stare. *How did I get so lucky?* Falyn had her hair down in ringlet curls arranged perfectly around her flawless face; her eyes were enhanced by just a hint of makeup, and her lips were glossed a rosy pink. She wore a loose-fitting white V-neck T-shirt tucked into dark blue skinny jeans that were stylishly weathered and worn in all the right places, along with a long sand-colored cardigan. Around her neck she wore a gold necklace with a silver dollar-sized pendant that rested on the swell of her cleavage and tall, brown leather boots that came almost to her knees, making her legs look long despite her petite stature. She looked the epitome of cool, casual, and it made Sylvio's mouth dry as he took her in.

"You look fantastic," he said, coming over to her and wrapping his arms around her shoulders.

"You only say that because you usually see me in black pants and a blouse or my chef's coat," she teased, hooking her arms around his neck and planting a chaste kiss on his lips. "It's nice not to dress in uniform for a change."

Sylvio laughed and looked down at himself. The usual tight T-shirt and jeans. "I guess I didn't get the memo."

Falyn volleyed his laugh and released him, not before giving his ass a firm squeeze and offering him a coquettish look. "I happen to be very fond of your jeans and what's in them."

"Woman, if you do that again, we aren't going anywhere. I'll just throw you over my shoulder caveman style and do wicked things to you in the bedroom.

"Later," she replied with a wink, looping her fingers into the belt loops of his jeans as she gazed up at him. "You have a long overdue date to bring me on and you haven't given me a single hint. C'mon, Sylvio, just a crumb, please."

Sylvio let out a bountiful laugh and replied. "All I will

say is I'm about to give you a glimpse into my childhood. We're going to take a trip down memory lane."

* * *

SYLVIO GREW up in the west end of Winnipeg near the army base. With his father in the military, they, like many other families, were housed in tiny cookie-cutter houses along a busy city street. Despite the small space and the tiny yard out back, Sylvio never felt stifled or lacking. The house was just big enough for the four of them and, between the school only a few blocks away, Sylvio and his brother, Antonio, always had enough room to run and play. Plus, with all the houses being military homes on their block, there were plenty of other kids to hang out with. His mother was often alone with her boys and made it her mission to look for ways to keep them active and out of trouble. One of the ways she did this was by taking them roller skating. Every Saturday, no matter what the weather, she would load them into her station wagon and off they went to the rink. She loved to roller skate, and very quickly they did too. It had become their favorite pastime, and when Sylvio thought back to the fun of those afternoons and the smile on his mother's face, he couldn't help but feel happy.

They pulled into the parking lot and up to the building, Falyn craning her neck to see the sign. "Skate it Easy". Is this a roller rink?"

Sylvio nodded. "This was my mother's favorite place to bring us when we were kids. Have you ever been?"

"I mean I've figure skated when I was a kid, but never

roller skated." She said with an eager smile as she unbuckled her seatbelt. "Can't be too hard, right?"

Sylvio smiled, appreciating her willingness to try something new, and got out of the SUV. Falyn followed suit as he took her hand, and they walked into the building together. The place was empty, and an elderly man, Falyn guessed to be in his mid-seventies, greeted them at the door.

"Sylvio!" he exclaimed, putting his hand out to greet him. "I was so surprised when you called me. I had to come see for myself that it was you."

"Thanks for opening it up for us today." Sylvio said, taking his offered hand, then turning to Falyn. "This is my girlfriend, Falyn."

"Girlfriend? Aren't you a little too old for a girlfriend, Sylvio?" the sweet senior teased. "Nice to meet you, Falyn. Such a pretty name for a pretty lady. I'm Fred, an old army buddy of Sylvio's late father." Falyn shook his hand as he smiled at her with kind brown eyes, weathered and wrinkled from a life well lived.

"Very nice to meet you, Fred. Do you own this place?"

"I do indeed. 35 years now. My home away from home," he said, smoothing down his snow-white hair. "Lots of memories at this old rink. Did Sylvio tell you he used to come here every weekend? It was his mother that convinced me to buy it and I never looked back," he said with nostalgia in his tone as he looked out towards the rink, before he turned back to Sylvio and Falyn.

"You two kids have fun. Grab your own skates, and the snack shack is open. This place is all yours this afternoon. I'll go cue up the music and the lights," he said, turning and slowly making his way to the booth attached to the rink.

Falyn turned to Sylvio, giving him an impressed look. "We have this place all to ourselves."

He nodded as "Ice Ice Baby" suddenly blared through the speakers and colorful oscillating spotlights criss-crossed the rink floor. Falyn laughed as Sylvio took her hand and led her to the counter where they stored the roller skates. Picking out their correct sizes, he led her to a bench where they put them on. Once laced up, Sylvio stood, taking both of Falyn's hands, lifting her from the bench, her stance precarious at first. Resting his hands on her waist, he steadied her. "Are you ready?" he asked.

"I think so," she replied, her smile wide as he held onto her, his arms wrapped around her waist as he guided her towards the rink. Carefully they stepped out, Falyn gripping tightly onto him to get her balance.

"I won't let you fall," he said, placing his hands on her waist as he skated backwards. She gripped his forearms, and he gave her a wink. "At least not more than you already have."

* * *

Meeting Sylvio's gaze, she gave him an appreciative smile. *He's being so damn cute today.* With the firm grip of his hands on her hips, they made one round; him skating backwards with her facing him, then changing positions, his hands on her waist behind her. The heat of his body behind her made her feel warm and safe, and soon her shoulders eased as she found a rhythm.

"You're doing so well," he complimented, skating up beside her.

"Thanks," she replied, glancing over to him, then doing a double take, realizing he was no longer holding onto her. With that realization she wobbled, and he was there taking her hand to help her regain her balance. Sliding his arms around her, they skated several rounds. The up-tempo music turned to a U2 Ballad as "With or Without You" blared from the speakers, and Falyn sighed, "I love this song." Sylvio nodded and grinned as she continued. "It's so beautiful and sad all in one. He's waiting for this woman he loves to come back to him, and he gives all of himself to her, but it's not enough. It kind of reminds me of my marriage in a way. I gave and gave and sacrificed to be with Pierre, but in the end, I was the one that came out battered and bruised. It was the hardest thing I've ever done, rebuilding my life."

"You did it though," he interjected with a proud smile. "Brilliantly, I might add."

Falyn squeezed his hand and offered him an appreciative look as she added. "It hasn't been easy."

"I hope I'm easing things for you by being there. I wasn't kidding when I said I wanted to invest in Prairie Charm. That includes my time. I would like to be a team."

"I'd like that," she beamed. "You know you're going to have a lot more time on your hands with selling The Pickled Pig. What do you plan on doing with all your time, other than helping me with Prairie Charm?"

"I don't know exactly. More dates with you, of course," he replied with a wink that made her grin. "I think I'll have more time to just enjoy life with you and whomever else comes along."

Falyn's eyes met his. *Is he talking about children?* The desire to have a child had been within her for years, but ever since she and Sylvio reunited, that ache had quelled into a deep, yearning pain. They had talked about children and had agreed they both wanted to experience parenthood together, but no timeline had been discussed, and Falyn wasn't about to pressure him. Not again. For now, her answer needed to be simple.

"I like the sound of that."

LEAVING THE ROLLER RINK, Falyn's hand in the back pocket of his jeans and his muscular arm around her shoulders, they made their way to his vehicle like two lovesick teenagers. "Oh, my God, that was so much fun," Falyn declared, her smile so big it made Sylvio's heart burst. "Where to next?"

"To my favorite diner of course," he replied, planting a quick kiss on her lips. "It's just outside the city and a place I used to go a lot as a teen. I can neither confirm nor deny bringing a few high school dates there."

"What were you like as a teenager? Were you the bad boy all the rebellious girls wanted to date?" she asked with a wiggle of her brows as she got into the vehicle and buckled her seat belt.

"I was a jock, actually. I played football all through junior high and high school, so it was more the promiscuous cheerleaders that had their eyes on me," he replied with a laugh.

"Not the other way around?" she asked cheekily.

"I never said that."

Falyn laughed, looking out the window as they exited the parking lot.

"What were you like in high school?" he asked with genuine curiosity in his tone.

Falyn turned to face him, a naughty smile curling her lips. "I was a bit of a rebel. Snuck out a lot, stayed up way past my curfew, had a few boyfriends. My parents don't know half of what I did, and they never will."

"Really?" he replied, a hint of surprise in his tone. She nodded and shrugged as he asked, "Any other make-out sessions on the back of motorcycles?"

"No, that was a first for me," she giggled.

"And the last," he countered.

"And the last," she agreed, reaching for his hand. "No, back then I was more into the bed of a truck or in a farmer's field kind of thing. Oh, and against a barn wall. You get creative in the country," she added, cocking a coy brow at him. "You had no idea I was a badass too, did you?"

"No, but I like it," he replied with a waggle of his brows. "Perhaps I can get a glimpse at the badass Falyn afterwards when I take you to an old make-out spot I know about."

"Why, Sylvio Conti, was that your plan all along, to get me into the backseat?" she inquired wickedly.

A slow smile curled his lips as he answered, his voice deep and growly, "I can neither confirm nor deny."

* * *

ARRIVING AT THEIR SECOND DESTINATION, Falyn couldn't help but grin at the 50s-style diner. The building was bright and cheerful, welcoming patrons to come in. Once inside, an authentic 1950s Jukebox, black and white checkerboard floors, shiny red vinyl booths, and Formica tabletops greeted them. A long countertop graced the front of the restaurant where your food was ordered, and all the employees were dressed in bowling-style shirts and visor caps.

"Hungry?" Sylvio asked as they stepped in line at the order counter.

"Yes," Falyn answered, her stomach taking that moment to growl.

Sylvio laughed, raising an eyebrow to her, "Do you trust me to order?"

Falyn nodded and went on tiptoe to plant a chaste kiss on his lips. "I'm going to find us a booth." Looking around the busy restaurant, she spotted a booth near the window, close to the jukebox. Claiming it, she slid onto the vinyl bench and glanced outside at the dimming light of day. Her cheeks hurt from smiling and laughter, her heart so full as sweet contentment fell over her. She wanted this feeling forever. To have days like this with Sylvio. Days where it didn't matter exactly what they did, as long as they were together and were happy. *Have I ever been this happy?* There wasn't even a need to ask. The answer was a resounding no.

When Sylvio returned, breaking her from her reflection with a tray carrying two tall juicy burgers, curly fries and two chocolate milkshakes, Falyn's stomach growled again at the delicious smelling food.

"I know it's not the caliber of what you cook, but sometimes you just want a good dirty cheeseburger," he said, slipping in beside her. "And dare I say this is one of the best burgers you are ever going to eat."

Falyn gave him a chiding look. "I might be a chef with a honed palate, but I can appreciate a good burger. Although I'm not sure much can beat the greasy goodness of the Eazy Café."

Sylvio set a large burger with a thick beef patty, loaded with lettuce, tomatoes, pickles and two large onion rings in front of her, and he gestured for her to go ahead. Eying the burger, she licked her lips. *It does look good.* Pressing the burger down with two hands, she picked it up and took a huge bite, letting ketchup smear the corner of her mouth. *Sweet Lord.* She let out a moan of approval, closed her eyes savoring that first meaty bite, and when she slowly opened them Sylvio was there, staring at her with a combination of amusement and appreciation.

"Just when I thought I couldn't love you more," he replied, leaning in and swiping the ketchup from the corner of her mouth with the tip of his tongue. His eyes met hers as he tucked a curl behind her ear, and the sizzling touch of his fingertips made Falyn's pulse quicken. Something so small, but every time Sylvio touched her, it was electric. Just like the night they met.

"I love you." She declared, meeting his gaze and bringing her hand up to caress the scruff of his chin. "You make me so happy."

"It's become my life's mission," he replied, picking up a curly fry and holding it out to her.

Falyn nabbed it with her teeth, playfully making Sylvio laugh before she did the same to him as he snarled and growled, then kissed her on the cheek. They continued their meal, feeding each other playfully until Falyn couldn't eat another bite.

"That was so good, but I'm so full," she said, easing back in the booth and resting her hand on her belly.

The sweet giggle of a little girl sounded, and both Sylvio and Falyn glanced towards the sound to see a little girl with wild blonde curls, around two years old, weaving between the tables and chairs. The little girl stopped in front of their booth and smiled up at them just as a young mother rounded the corner, spotting her daughter. The little girl stared at them with big blue eyes as the mother caught up to her. Sylvio plucked a leftover curly fry from their tray and looked up at the mother for her permission. She nodded, and he leaned down, putting it out for the little girl to grab. The little girl took it from him carefully, smiled sweetly and eagerly stuffed it into her mouth.

"Sorry, I turned my back for a moment, and she was off and running. I'm sorry if she disturbed you," the mother said with an exasperated look.

"She didn't disturb us at all." Falyn replied with a smile. "How old is she?"

The mother scooped up the little girl, holding her on her hip as she answered, "2 years old and a handful, but I wouldn't trade it for anything." she said, planting a kiss on the little girl's cheek before walking off with the adorable little girl in her arms.

As Falyn watched them go, those familiar pangs returned with vengeance, and this time Falyn needed to know where they stood on a timeline for starting a family. But before she could broach the subject, Sylvio declared, "Let's do that, Falyn."

Falyn stared at him. *Is he being serious?* Looking away for a moment, she took a deep breath and let it out slowly, trying to sort out her thoughts and figure out what she wanted to say. "Sylvio, we broke up once because I wanted to know where things were going with us. And although I think we're on the same page now with the conversations we've had. I need clarification. And I'm sorry if that makes me come across as impatient or demanding. It's just when I think of forever you are always in it and when I think of who the father to my future children will be, you're always the one I see. I want all of it with you, Sylvio. The marriage, the children, everything, and if you were to ask me when, I'd say now. I'm ready, but are you?"

* * *

THIS WAS THE MOMENT. Falyn had been patient, giving them the time they needed and supportively standing beside him as he got his closure from the past. Without responding to her question, Sylvio slid out of the booth and walked over to the jukebox, her eyes following curiously. Pulling some loose change from his pocket, he inserted the coins, feeling her eyes boring into his back as he made his selection. A Percy Sledge classic came through loud and clear as the opening of "When a Man Loves a Woman" belted through the speakers. He turned to face her, and a smile teased her lips as he sauntered back over to their booth and put out his hand.

"Dance with me?" he asked, meeting her gaze, both expectant and a little confused.

She took his hand as she slid out of the booth, and he led her to a space in front of the jukebox, drawing the attention of other patrons as he twirled her, making her giggle and pulled her into him. The warmth of her body against his, her hand resting gently on his heart. Everything he wanted from this day forward and for the rest of his life was right here in his arms. He gazed down at the woman who had captured his heart and made him believe in love again. His hand settled on hers, and in that moment, he never wanted this feeling to end. The exquisitely perfect feeling of loving someone so completely and knowing they are the one and only person meant for you. They swayed to the music, time and place fading around them. Just the two of them and this moment. Looking deep into her miraculous brown eyes, her love shone back at him, honest and pure. He couldn't wait. Not a moment longer. His soul calling out to hers as he spoke.

"Falyn, before I met you, I never thought it was possible to find love again, and I had resigned myself to the fact that I would be alone for the rest of my life. And then, like an angel falling from the sky, there you were. And all it took was one look into your eyes and the shackles around my heart broke away, allowing you inside. I want to spend the rest of my life making your dreams come true, and that includes a happy, faithful marriage and a beautiful family. I don't want to wait another second to do this." With that, Sylvio lowered to one knee, reached into the inside pocket of his leather jacket and pulled out a blue velvet box, opening it to reveal a beautiful gold band with a single halo-cut diamond. Something that matched the beauty of the woman standing before him.

"Sylvio," Falyn whispered breathlessly, as he looked up at her questioning.

"Will you marry me, Angel?"

Tears welled up in her eyes, and with a tremble in her voice, she answered on a breath, "Yes, I will marry you. I love you so much, Sylvio."

Pure joy filled Sylvio's heart, and he closed his eyes for a beat, relishing her response, her hands finding his hair and feathering through it. Emotion rose to the surface as he opened his eyes, her loving gaze glistening with happy tears as she leaned down and kissed him tenderly, repeating her answer against his lips. "Yes."

Rising to his feet, he took out the ring, placing it on her finger, before the restaurant erupted in applause, cheers and whistles. Sylvio laughed, Falyn too, as he scooped her into his arms and swung her around. Falyn giggled, throwing her head back in joyous laughter as she held out her hand, admiring the beautiful ring on her finger.

"How about we get out of here and go to that make out place I told you about?" he asked, whispering into her ear before pulling back to gaze into her eyes.

With a cocked brow and a coquettish wink, she replied, "I thought you'd never ask."

* * *

THE SUV WINDOWS WERE FOGGED; the intense heat inside the vehicle causing a sheen of sweat to cover them both as Falyn rode out her pleasure, Sylvio buried deep inside her body. "I fucking love my fiancé," he growled out huskily, as she undulated her body over him, his large palms cupping and squeezing her breasts with each grind and press.

"Call me that again," she cried out, her body tightening around his hard steel length.

"My fiancé," he repeated with a moan. "I'm going to marry you and put a baby inside you, oh fuck Falyn tell me you're there as I'm about to…fuck…" he managed between heavy breaths. Falyn's eyes met his, their chocolate brown depths hazy with lust and full of love as their bodies gave into the pleasure. A profound moment of pure desire and promise between two lost souls that found each other. Through all the hurt, betrayal, and tragedy, they were brought together by the universe to help each other heal and to get a second chance at the life they always wanted.

As they came down from the pinnacle, bodies trembling, slick sweat clinging to them, Sylvio brushed the curls from her beautifully flushed face and drew her to him, kissing her lips tenderly. Tears pricked his eyes; a raw, intense emotion filled his chest, and he let out a stuttered breath. Falyn, as if reading his emotions, laid her head on his shoulder, her hot breath on his neck as they held each other, letting their feelings overflow. Running his fingers over her bare back, her body melted into his, the last remnants of the pain of their pasts evaporating into the steamy air around them.

CHAPTER 16

As spring came to Primrose, Sylvio's final days as owner of The Pickled Pig drew near. Sylvio shared the news with his staff first. There were some tears, many of his staff having been with him for years, most of them having become like family. But when they found out it was his son that he was passing the torch to, they were not only surprised but thrilled. The Pickled Pig would live on, even without Sylvio at the helm.

Two weeks before possession, Thatcher flew to Manitoba, not only to introduce himself to the staff but to find a place to live and set up boarding for his horse. Despite this big change, it had become evident to Sylvio that his son wasn't about to give up on his cowboy status.

"I still am a little perplexed why you decided to uproot yourself completely, move provinces, leave your career and buy my bar?" Sylvio asked, leaning back in his office chair. Thatcher sat across from him, a slow smile curling his lips.

"Well, if I'm being honest, there wasn't much for me in

Smoky Lake and the more I came out here, between my friends and you, it felt like the right move. Then when my dad mentioned you were going to sell The Pickled Pig, it seemed like the perfect opportunity," he said, leaning forward and resting his elbows on the desk. "Since this is my first business, is it too presumptuous to ask if I can come to you for advice from time to time? I know you'll be busy with Prairie Charm, but any wisdom you can pass on will be appreciated."

"Son, you know anytime you need advice about anything, you can come to me. Business, love, anything at all."

Thatcher smiled, giving Sylvio a grateful look before he leaned back in his chair and pinned him with an amused gaze. "Speaking of love, I couldn't help but notice the rock you put on Falyn's finger. When's the date?"

"No date set yet. Honestly between selling the Pig and things picking up for the spring and summer season at Prairie Charm we haven't decided on anything yet." Sylvio replied. "It will be soon though; I've waited a long time for someone like her to come into my life and I can't wait to marry her and have a family."

* * *

FALYN HUNG UP THE PHONE, her heart bursting.

"That's a bright smile," Sylvio commented, leaning on the kitchen counter at the guest house.

"That was my brother. He and Georgie are finally getting married. Two weeks from now, the location of the ceremony will remain a secret until an hour before the wedding."

"That sounds fun."

Falyn nodded, her smile growing wider. "They want to have the reception here. Our first wedding reception here at Prairie Charm."

"That's exciting," Sylvio replied. "Speaking of weddings, I've been thinking a lot about the back lawn and the space there. What do you think about transforming that space into a place for outdoor weddings? We can put in a garden, perhaps a gazebo. It would be perfect for an outdoor ceremony space and pictures. There is also enough space to have a tent set up for outdoor receptions, which I assume is what we'll have set up for Brooks and Georgie. Then in winter we can offer indoor weddings. The great room would be perfect for ceremonies and easy to transform for a reception."

"I like the idea, and have considered it myself, but being a one-person show, it was hard to figure out how to execute the vision," Falyn shared. "But now with you here and putting your resources in, I think we can make it happen."

"I will talk to a guy Hayden introduced me to, Wilder Bryant. He's a landscaper. He just opened his own business, and I've seen his work. He's amazing," he said. "But first we can talk to Jaxon. I need to talk to him about renovating the cottage and getting that going this summer if possible. We're going to need the space."

"You better get on that. I have a feeling it won't be long," Falyn said, placing her hand on her belly. Sylvio rounded the island, his arms coming around her and settling over her hand.

"I can't wait to see you with my child," he whispered against her ear, his breath hot and making her core pulse for him. "Big belly. Even bigger…"

Sylvio cupped her breasts and squeezed gently, Falyn squirming away laughing. "Get out of my kitchen!" she exclaimed playfully, swatting him away. "I have a wedding reception to plan, and you have some phone calls to make."

* * *

LEANING BACK IN HER TUB, Falyn sighed, her mood causing a dark cloud to cover her today. She hadn't told Sylvio yet; the disappointment was too much at the moment. For now, she had to soak. Soak her worries and disappointment away. It was late, after midnight, and she couldn't sleep, not without the heat of Sylvio at her back and his body curled around hers. She couldn't wait until he went to bed with her every night. No more late nights at the Pig. She closed her eyes, willing away negative thoughts and trying to replace them with hopeful ones.

The lock on the front door disengaged. Falyn opened her eyes. Sylvio appeared before her, leaning against the doorframe of the bathroom, his brows drawn together in concern.

"Can't sleep? Do you need tea or perhaps a glass of wine?" he asked, ready to fetch her whatever her heart desired.

"Wine, please."

Sylvio's eyes flitted over to the bathroom counter where the pregnancy test sat, and he didn't need to pick it up to know the result.

"I'm sorry, Angel," he said, kneeling down by the tub and smoothing the wet curls from her face, then leaning in and planting a kiss on her lips. "These things can take time, and the wait will be worth it, I promise you."

Falyn nodded, and Sylvio rose to his feet, exiting the bathroom to get her a glass of wine. She was being silly. Thinking back to the beginning of her relationship with Sylvio, she had been impatient, wanting to know where they were going and when. It wasn't until she put her impatience aside and they decided to try again that their relationship started to flourish. Now they were engaged, committing to marry and trying to start a family. She needed to stop putting pressure on things and just enjoy this time together.

Entering the bathroom again, Sylvio handed her a glass of wine and, as if reading her mind, he started stripping off his clothes. Her eyes followed his movements as he climbed into the tub behind her, cradling her body, his arms around her protectively, and his soothing deep voice in her ear. "Be patient, my angel. It'll be worth the wait."

* * *

TEARS OF JOY filled Fallon's eyes as she watched her brother, Brooks, vow his eternal love to his childhood best friend and love of his life, Georgie Donahue. These two had been to hell and back in the past two years, with Georgie fighting and beating a rare form of breast cancer and Brooks standing beside her as her rock and foundation through it all.

Now as she watched them sway on the dance floor, under twinkling fairy lights with the prairie sunset as a backdrop, so deeply in love and so completely perfect for each other, all of her worries seemed trite. If her brother could wait and be patient, so could she.

Strong muscular arms came around her waist, and Falyn leaned back, inhaling Sylvio's soothing scent.

"That could be us soon," he murmured against her ear. "Have you considered a date yet?"

Falyn turned in his arms, hooking her wrists at his neck as she went on her tiptoes and met his gaze. "I know this might seem a bit cheesy, but what about a Christmas wedding? Just something small and simple here at Prairie Charm. In front of the hearth. A beautifully decorated Christmas tree in the background. I know it's a little cliché romantic, but it would be so beautiful."

A slow smile curled Sylvio's lips. "It sounds perfect to me."

* * *

JUST LIKE THE old saying goes, good things come to those who wait, and the next six months proved this to be true. It was their wedding day, Christmas Day, the snow outside kissing the trees with sparkling hoar frost, making it look like a magical winter wonderland. Prairie Charm was ready for the onslaught of celebration, decked to the nines in lavish evergreen garland with trims of red and gold. Everything was just as Falyn had dreamed, and yet, it wasn't the Hallmark worthy décor or the beauty of the winter day outside that had her beaming. It was the positive pregnancy test in her hands.

She had a feeling she was pregnant, but she chalked up her exhaustion and upset stomach to stress due to wedding preparations. Too many months of back-to-back disappointment had thickened her skin and settled her resolve. It wasn't until her period uncharacteristically didn't make its monthly appearance that she finally believed it to be true. She smoothed her hand over her midriff and closed her eyes, tears escaping through her lashes, and she started to laugh. A joyous laugh surged through her body.

"Are you okay in there?" the voice of her sister-in-law, Georgie, asked through the bathroom door.

"Yes," Falyn giggled, holding the test to her chest. "I'm just so happy!"

Georgie laughed on the other side of the door, "Fair enough, as you should be on your wedding day. We do need to get ready, though. The ceremony is in an hour, and Brooks texted me that Sylvio is going to wear out the soles of his shoes with all his pacing if we don't get there on time. He's so anxious."

I need to tell Sylvio. A thought passed through her mind, and a slow grin curved up her lips. Tucking the test into her robe pocket, she opened the bathroom door to find Georgie there, her brown eyes sparkling with mirth. "Do you think you could deliver a gift to Sylvio before the ceremony?"

* * *

SYLVIO PACED in front of the hearth, the guests starting to gather in the great room. Less than an hour till the ceremony and Sylvio was nearly vibrating with anticipation at the thought of his angel walking down the aisle towards him. He had waited a lifetime for this woman, and he didn't want to wait a moment longer than necessary to call her his wife.

Suddenly Georgie appeared, her cheeks rosy from the cold outside, dressed in her bridesmaid dress, and her eyes sparkling with delight. She went on her tiptoes and planted a chaste kiss on Brooks lips before he noticed the little gift bag in her hands. Striding over to Sylvio, she met his curious gaze and leaned in whispering. "Falyn wanted me to give this to you. But she said you needed to open it alone. Not in front of everyone."

Sylvio nodded, taking the bag from her hands as he excused himself and slipped outside onto the back patio. The frigid December cold bit at his skin, but he paid it no mind as he reached into the bag and pulled out a note card. Opening the envelope, he read:

My dearest Sylvio,

The day we've been waiting for is finally here. A day you and I commit our lives to one another, and I become your wife. I can't wait to call you, my husband. Meet us in one hour in front of that fireplace. Because I'm about to marry the heck out of you.

All my love, Falyn

Sylvio smiled, going to tuck the notecard back into the envelope, before his eyes caught on one small detail. *Meet us?* Sylvio's brows knitted together in confusion as he dug his hand in the bag and pulled out a stick-like object. His eyes grew wide as his brain caught up to what he was holding. Opening his large palm, he looked down, and in his hand was a pregnancy test, the word 'pregnant' on the little screen. Instant tears pricked Sylvio's eyes as he stared down at the test, a low rumble reverberating from his chest as laughter escaped his lips. Pure, boisterous laughter. *Falyn is pregnant! I'm going to be a father!* The patio door cracked open, and Thatcher, in his signature black cowboy hat, popped his head outside, an amused look on his face.

"Dad, are you okay? I mean if you're losing your shit out here, with all due respect I get it. I'd be too if I were the one getting married. But I think you're scaring your guests with that laugh," Thatcher informed by gesturing with his thumb behind him. Sylvio looked over his shoulder to see all eyes trained on him, with a combination of curiosity and mirth and, in some cases, utter confusion.

Stuffing the pregnancy test back into the bag, Sylvio followed Thatcher back inside. All the guests had arrived and settled into their seats. Thatcher and Antonio stood by Sylvio's side as a beautiful, petite young woman with wispy, shoulder-length dark brown hair and big, beautiful brown eyes stepped forward, wearing a simple green dress and guitar in her hand.

An elbow nudged Sylvio in the side, and he turned to see Thatcher, his eyes locked on the young woman. "Who's that?"

"Rose," Sylvio replied.

"Rose," Thatcher echoed, his eyes transfixed as the young woman smiled at the guests and started to play, the gentle strum of her guitar filling the room. Rose began to sing, the unique rasp of her smoky voice delivering the first line of "When a Man Loves a Woman." *Their song.* Sylvio glanced at his son next to him, a smile tugging at his lips. He knew that look. The same look he had when he met Falyn.

The guests turned their gazes to the end of the aisle as Georgie and Brooks walked down the aisle together, Maid and Man of Honor. They offered Sylvio each a nod and a smile as the guests rose to their feet. His eyes drifted to the end of the aisle, where his Angel stood. Adorned in lace cap sleeves, plunging into a sweetheart neckline and drifting down to a delicate dress made of intricate ivory lace. She looked like a dream. *My dream.* A beautiful angel with a halo of dark blonde curls that were swept up, ringlets kissing her gorgeous face that was dusted with light makeup, allowing her beloved freckles to shine through. Her rosy glossed lips curled into a smile as she hooked her arm into her father's, and they made their way down the aisle. Duncan's chin high and proud, her expressive eyes dancing with pure, unbridled happiness.

Hot tears pricked Sylvio's eyes, and he blinked, swallowing down the swell of emotion catching in his throat. Seeing her walking towards him, the woman he waited for what felt like a lifetime for, the woman that was carrying his child, opened the floodgates. Tears spilled onto his cheeks, and he pulled out the handkerchief stuffed into the front pocket of his suit jacket, dabbing at his face. Falyn beamed as they reached him, and he stepped forward, Duncan placing her hand in his. Symbolically passing the torch as her protector to Sylvio.

With a final clap on Sylvio's back, Duncan took his seat in the front row, next to Dorothy, who was already crying and sniffling into a tissue.

"Hey there, silver fox," she said, reaching up and catching a tear left on his cheek. "We're here as promised."

Sylvio's eyes drifted down to her stomach where she rested her hand and back up to meet her eyes, pure joy and happiness in their depths. "Are you ready for this?" he asked. "To spend a lifetime with this tattooed, motorcycle-riding bad boy."

Falyn reached up and cupped his face with her palm tenderly as she replied. "There's no one I'd rather spend my life with."

There, in front of the beautiful hearth at Prairie Charm Bed and Breakfast, surrounded by everyone who loved and supported them, Falyn and Sylvio committed their lives to each other. Two broken souls that were drawn together by fate waded through all the mess and muck of the past and found a beautiful love story together.

That night as they held each other, naked, their bodies satiated, hearts full, and their spirits blissfully happy. Sylvio placed his large, warm palm on her stomach and sighed contentedly into her hair. "One day down…"

Falyn met his steely gaze, smiling dreamily, "And forever to go."

EPILOGUE

Five years later

The scene was set. The stockings hung by the fireplace with care, as a crackling fire kicked up embers drifting up into the chimney. The tall Douglas fir sat in the corner, decorated in a menagerie of popsicle stick ornaments, gold-painted pinecones strung with red string, and construction paper creations depicting Rudolph and Santa Claus. Brightly wrapped gifts underneath the tree, just a sampling of what was yet to come when Santa's sleigh finally arrived.

Their four-year-old fraternal twins, Frankie and Marco sat on a blanket a safe distance from the fire, clad in matching Christmas jammies, their favorite stuffies snuggled into their laps enjoying the warmth along with mugs of hot chocolate and a shared plate of Christmas cookies.

Sylvio entered the room carrying two more steaming mugs and handed one carefully to Falyn. She smiled at her handsome silver fox husband, who was now more salt than pepper. *Raising rambunctious little ones will do that to you,* she thought, fingering a blonde curl that now included hints of grey. He looked good, though. Still the hot, muscular, motorcycle-riding bad boy she married five years ago, although now he mostly drove a minivan. Sylvio's blue-grey eyes danced with the light of the fireplace as he settled in beside her, draping his arm casually around her shoulder and giving it a squeeze. She glanced up at him, and he gave her his sultry bedroom eyes, knowing full well that her husband had plans for them once the kids were in bed tonight. Although Sylvio was approaching 60, his age didn't match his libido, and Falyn was a wholly satisfied woman.

"Who's all joining us for dinner tomorrow night?" Sylvio asked, taking a careful sip of his hot chocolate.

"Mom, Dad, Brooks, Georgie, their girls and of course little Roan," she replied, beaming at the thought of holding her brother's newborn son. "Thatcher and his crew, Antonio and Suzanne, and of course my parents."

"Mama?" Frankie said, turning to face them, her blonde curls bouncing with the turn of her head and her big brown eyes filled with concern. "How does Santa get down the chimney? Won't he burn his butt?"

Marco giggled beside her, repeating the word 'butt' as he turned to face them on the couch. His blue-grey eyes and dark hair made him look so much like his big brother, Thatcher, it was uncanny. Sylvio leaned forward, capturing her gaze, and grinned. "Santa is like a magician. All he has to do is sprinkle a little magic down the chimney and poof!" Sylvio popped open his fingers. "The fire goes out."

Frankie's eyes twinkled with wonder as she smiled. Marco, however, was not to be fooled. He rolled his eyes adorably and pinned Sylvio with his intense stare. "You are so weird, Dad. Everyone knows Santa sends down snow to put out the fire, not magic. It's science."

Sylvio held his hands up before leaning back onto the couch with a smirk as he leaned in and whispered in Falyn's ear from the corner of his mouth. "What are our children learning in preschool?"

Falyn chuckled, whispering her reply, "Science apparently."

Soon the fire ebbed, just smoldering bits of ash left, and Frankie and Marco lay snuggled up on their blanket, with Sylvio and Falyn, their eyes half-mast staring into the light glow of the hearth that still remained.

"Do you think it's safe to bundle them up and carry them back to the cottage?" Falyn asked.

"They're out, Angel," he confirmed, rising from the couch and glancing over at their angelic faces.

Snuffing out the rest of the fire, they quickly cleaned up, covertly adding a handful of presents under the tree marked from Santa and together they each scooped up a child, bundling them in their blankets as they carried them across the snowy driveway to the cottage.

Although their home had now doubled in size with them adding an extra floor for the twins' bedrooms, their cottage still was as quaint and cute as it was when Falyn first moved in. Although the space could still be considered small to some, it was the perfect size for their little family.

Unlocking the door, they shucked off their boots and jackets, then made their way up the stairs to the twins' bedrooms. Marco clung to Falyn and Frankie to her daddy as they went to their respective rooms and placed them in bed. As Falyn always did, she draped Marco's baby blanket over his shoulders and brushed the dark hair from his handsome little face. Marco's eyes drifted open, heavy with sleep, their blue-grey color sparkling in the dim lamplight. "I love you, mama," he said as a sweet smile curled his lips and he drifted back to sleep. Falyn smiled down at her sweet little boy. A child she hoped and prayed for and that came into her life exactly when she was ready. A child so worth the wait.

"Falyn." Sylvio's deep, low voice sounded from behind her, breaking her from her reflection as he put his hand on her shoulder. "Frankie's waiting for you."

Falyn affectionately covered her husband's hand, gave it a squeeze, then rose, turning back just in time to see Sylvio affectionately kiss their son's head. As suspected, Sylvio's dad game was strong.

Entering her daughter's room, Frankie's half-mast brown eyes gleamed in the lamplight as she put her arms out for a hug. Falyn leaned in and hugged her, her sweet little fingers playing with the curls at the nape of Falyn's neck. As she was about to release her daughter and tuck her into bed, Frankie's gaze pinned her with deep, intense sincerity as she said, "Please tell Santa I'm sorry for hitting Marco."

Falyn stifled a laugh as she replied. "Okay, baby girl. I love you."

"Love you too, Mama," Frankie responded with a breath as she closed her sleepy eyes.

Falyn rose from her bed, an amused smile still on her face as she turned to see Sylvio leaning against the door frame, legs crossed at the ankles, looking like the sexiest Christmas present ever.

Sauntering across the room, Falyn gently closed her daughter's bedroom door as she stepped into the hallway, turned to face her husband and crooked her finger at him coquettishly. Sylvio's eyes darkened, pure lust causing his jaw to tick. She knew that look. That look meant only one thing. "You know, it's after midnight and technically our anniversary. Is the silver fox on the prowl?"

A low growl escaped his lips as he stalked over to her and swooped her up over his shoulder, caveman style. She let out a tiny squeal, hyperaware of the sleeping kids just a door away. Carrying her down the stairs, he didn't stop until they were in their bedroom and the door was locked behind them. Sylvio tossed her playfully onto the bed, his broad muscular body coming over her in an instant, hovering hot and heavy.

"Hi," Sylvio said, his face radiating love and devotion for his wife.

"Hi," she replied, running her hands through his silver locks.

"Angel, I'm so grateful you walked into my bar," Sylvio said, capturing her with his mesmerizing blue-grey eyes. "You were worth the wait."

She smiled, her heart full to bursting with love for her

adoring husband as she pulled him in for a passionate kiss then eased away ever so slight murmuring against his lips, "As were you."

* * *

Thank you for reading Prairie Charm!
Want more steamy romance set in the idyllic small town of Primrose?
Read Prairie Rose now!

ALSO BY TANYA RENEE

Primrose Series

Prairie Sky

Prairie Nights

Prairie Fire

Prairie Hearts

Prairie Sound

Prairie Rain

Prairie Prestige

Prairie Roads

Prairie Charm

Prairie Rose

With The Band

Finding Direction

Love Notes

On The Edge Of Forever

MORE FROM SERENADE PUBLISHING

Songbird series

By Sarah Williams

Songbird

Heartbeat Song

Our Song

Brigadier Station Series

By Sarah Williams:

The Brothers of Brigadier Station

The Sky over Brigadier Station

The Legacies of Brigadier Station

Christmas at Brigadier Station

Heart of the Hinterland Series

By Sarah Williams:

The Dairy Farmer's Daughter

Their Perfect Blend

Beyond the Barre

The Outback Governess

The Tooth Fairy Chronicles

By Victoria Rocus

Tooth Decay With A Side Of Fae

Toothaches And Wedding Cakes

Baby Tooth And Tangled Roots

Wisdom Tooth And The Awful Truth

Toothpicks And Wicked Tricks

Missing Teeth And What Lies Beneath

Toothless Grins And His Father's Sins

The Spring of Love Series

By Virginia Taylor

Forever Delighted

Forever Amused

Forever Heartfelt

ACKNOWLEDGMENTS

Book nine in the Primrose Series is here, and although this series isn't over yet it's hard to believe it's only been three years since I sat down at the kitchen table with my laptop and started writing the first book. As always, I am forever grateful to Sarah Williams from Serenade Publishing for seeing something in me that for many years I struggled to see in myself. A person who believes deeply in human connection and love and wants to share stories that reflect that. Thank you for giving me a shot at this whole author thing! You and your team are simply the best!

To my readers, what can I say. You are the reason this series has become so loved. Your enthusiasm reflected in your posts, messages, videos, reviews has given me so much validation. I appreciate every single kindness and word and because of that I want to strive to become a better writer as well as share more stories that resonate and touch your hearts. Thank you will never be enough.

Again, I need to thank my hometown of Landmark, Manitoba, for being the inspiration for Primrose and specifically for this book the inspiration for Prairie Charm Bed and Breakfast. Although this location is fictional, if you are from my hometown, you will know exactly where it's located. Love that you all enjoy my little, small town easter eggs!

Thank you to my dear friend Mandi, whom I dedicated this book to. When I told you I wanted to write an age gap romance with a sexy silver fox you were the first person to say, heck yeah! I hope you fall in love with Sylvio as much as I have! So grateful for your friendship and unfailing support! Hugs!

To my husband who never gets jealous of all my book boyfriends and who is my biggest supporter and champion. You will always be my dream man! Love you, Bart!

To my kids, two of the coolest people in the world, thank you for tolerating all my book talk with minimal eye rolls! Love you two so much!

And lastly thank you to my parents for instilling in me my resilient work ethic. And specifically, to my mom for always keeping it real. Sorry for all the sex scenes.

www.ingramcontent.com/pod-product-compliance
Lightning Source LLC
LaVergne TN
LVHW090935080826
845145LV00003B/758

* 9 7 8 1 7 6 4 0 6 4 6 4 4 *